His Assassin

Heather Morris

Contents

Chapter 1 ~ The Mission

'Kill The Alpha' and with that the call that had woken me up was ended and my phone buzzed with a message.

Death Assassin,

This is your mission, you will be going to LA to kill the Alpha there and his pack, his name is Sebastian Ezra. He is causing our company a lot of problems, so end it!

Your name is still Angel and you will be 18 but you will be joining the school there, as his beta is still in school get close to him, you will be living on your own 'because you want more independence'.

You will go tomorrow to leave your mark and buy a new house before the mission starts so don't let anyone catch you until you go to school, you have a week to get situated but you have 2 months of the mission otherwise i'll send help if you can't get the job done.

Don't draw attention to yourself!

Boss

Well that was pleasant, getting up i put on some leggings and a jumper before heading to the contact store just over the road. Walking in the lady who owned the store welcomed me.

"Back again Angel?" the old lady laughs already getting the contacts out for me.

"Yes ma'am" looking at the options while nodding my greeting to the old store owner.

"please go for the brown this time, i love your eye colour but i'd love to see you in brown" she pleads, she does this every time i always come here for contacts for a mission and she always tells me to go brown. Now there's nothing wrong with brown but normally i get given a colour by the boss but this time he didn't say so i nod my head and she squeals making me laugh.

Grabbing a beautiful hazel colour she gets them ready for me to try on, when they were in i open my eyes in front of the big mirror while she stood behind me. Instead of my normal eyes that were a dark blue around the outer circle, a crystal blue inside with patches of browns and gold hues they were the prettiest shade of hazel.

"Oh dear they look beautiful" she gasps clapping.

I pay for the contacts and she wishes me well, she's such a cheerful lady .

I saw a small brown package in front of my door when I reached my apartment, rolling my eyes i pick it up and head inside while cutting it open and just as i expected inside was my new passport, driving licence and my birth certificate for the school. They must have asked the lady what colour eye contacts i got because on it i had brown eyes with my normal white hair.

On all the documents my name was Angel Rose but on my real birth certificate Rose is just my middle name, my full name was Angel Rose Blackwood.

The boss knew no matter how hard he tried i would never change my hair because it reminded me of my mother.

I remember her and my father like it was yesterday, i was six and was getting ready for bedtime, my mother was reading to me. Her voice was like an angels, she sat next to me with her white hair tied up in a messy bun at the top of her head and she had on her night shorts and shirt.

My father had already given me a kiss goodnight, i remember his dark brown hair being messy and his stubble gently grazing my head as he kissed my forehead goodnight. His eyes which i got from him sparkled with love as he walked downstairs to finish the cleaning before bed.

My mother had started reading to me and i felt my eyes start to close when the quiet night was broken by my fathers screams of pain and the noises of fighting, i was so scared and looked at my mother in fear but she just closed the book and ripped me out of bed taking me to my wardrobe.

In the bottom of my wardrobe they had placed a bunker, in there was snacks and drinks, pillows and blankets for an emergency, placing me inside she pushed my hair off my face.

"Listen to me Angel, when i close this door do not come out no matter what you hear! Tomorrow i want you to go to LA and find Luca O'Connor he was my old Alpha and he will look after you. Remember that Angel, Luca O'Connor"

I remember nodding my head and grabbing onto her arm, she disconnected our hands and hers when to her neck. She took off the necklace my father got her for her birthday with our family portrait inside, placing it around my neck she kissed me and told me she loved me before closing the door.

I heard her crying and my door open and close, not long after i heard yelling and my mother's screams and yells from downstairs. I was crying at that point and gripping my teddy close to my face to smother the sounds.

There was footsteps coming to my room and i got quiet, the next thing i knew someone was trashing the house because of the smashing and yelling, Someone had emptied the wardrobe of everything in it but they wouldn't find me because the bunker was really hidden.

The next morning i left and saw my room and house smashed up but didn't see my parents anywhere, i packed a small bag because even at the age of 6 i wasn't silly, my parents had trained me well and because i was a werewolf, shocker, my wolf knew what to do.

Not long after Luca O'Connor found me not the other way around, and he wasn't an Alpha so i don't know if my mother had him mixed up but he took me to his company and trained me to be the best Assassin ever and that's what i did, from then on i was known as Death Assassin.

He promised me that he would find the people that took my parents and let me kill them. I felt in my bones my parents wasn't dead i just had to find them. Not long after my training was finished i became the best Assassin and i kept getting better over the 12 years i have been fighting, i was now 18 and he still haven't found them but i won't lose hope.

My last name died with them disappearing that day, as Luca said people would be after me as well if i used that so i changed it to my middle name, Luca also told me to only call him Boss which was weird but Alphas do that all the time?

I came back to reality and shook my head, 12 years and the people who took my parents are still walking around freely but not for long because this year i was going to looking on my own.

I grabbed my suitcases and started filling them up with clothes and all that jazz, i was going to get my weapons and camera equipment while in LA because i couldn't travel with them.

This mission was going to be long i could just tell.

Chapter 2 ~ Lone Wolf

A week later and I had already finished three small missions i was given in LA, in the assassin world there are three different types of missions, the first one is the one day mission where you're given a person, time and place when you got there you were expected to kill that person.

The second mission is one that could takes a few days, two weeks at the most and the last mission is ones that could take years but the faster you get it done the more you get paid.

So in LA i was doing three extra missions as well as my main one which was fun but it also gave me a chance to leave my mark.

A mark is like an assassin's signature, mine was a burn mark on my victims body in the letters DA standing for Death Assassin. Most people don't know how i do this but my father was a werewolf like me. However, my mother was a fire witch.

Now this may be confusing, you have a normal witch but then you have witches that are better with certain things, fire witches are better with fire if you hadn't guessed and i ended up getting that trait from my mother which i used to burn my victims.

The house i brought was just a basic house and i had already started unpacking but now i was going to start putting up my cameras.

Starting with the front of the house i fixed up the cameras and not long after i could look everywhere in my new house from just my bedroom.

I had also added a sensor camera into the front and back of my house as werewolves can be quiet but even they couldn't cheat a sensor camera, that was also hooked up to my room and i got a notification whenever it picked something up.

When i was certain everything was in it's place i went over each room again making sure everything was good, no one knew this but i had a secret obsession with the colour grey and baby pink, i know girlie for an assassin but i can't help it.

No one also knew that i had a puppy he was a German Shepard and he was fully grown but he was a huge boy for his breed, his head coming up to my waist at him standing normal but if he jumped up he stood over my tiny frame.

He was my baby and he knew it, i named him Cooper and he was the one thing i loved most in the world.

Reaching the kitchen i noticed how bare the cupboards were, shaking my head i grabbed coopers lead.

"Cooper!" i shout and not long after hear a thud from my room upstairs, that's one thing about Cooper he loved my bed and no matter how much i spent on a dog bed he'd just look at it like you buy it you sleep in it.

i smile when he runs around the corner, "hey baby" gently stroking his fur and he barks spotting the lead.

"Alright, time to go get food" i laugh at the silly pup in front of me, I've had Cooper for his whole life when I found him two years ago, someone had dumped him on the side of the road and every since he was mine, his still a puppy in my eyes and he'll still be my puppy when his 10.

The shops weren't a long way away and Cooper love the outdoors so we were both happy, but when we reached the shops i walked passed two boys and take notice that they smelt like werewolves.

Just as i took notice so did they.

"Rouge!" they growl luckily there was no humans nearby.

"Will you be quiet! I'm not a rouge" i say shaking my head and they get quiet.

"Why wasn't we told you were coming on our territory then?" the guy that i saw on my files as the Beta stated claws still out. He was William Spencer Owens the Alpha's childhood best friend they have been inseparable since birth, 6'0, brown eyes with brown hair he was a pretty much bob standard guy who gets good grades and plays football. Not much to say apart from he has a human mate, Summer Slade, this wasn't unheard of just rare.

"I'm not associated with a pack but the council haven't stated me as a rouge"

The council were a group of snobby werewolves who act like everyone was below them, they are like the 'leaders' of the werewolves but they weren't, the moon goddess was, however you can not be claimed as rouge unless you were taken to the council.

The council address the situation and decided if you deserve being claimed as a rouge, rouges were the lowest of the low, they're the people that rape, murder, kidnap you name it.

However if you run away from your pack you're just claimed as a lone wolf, these are people that can roam freely where ever they wish as long as they don't cause trouble.

"You're a lone wolf?" the guy that i have also read up on Niko Theodore White, 6'2, blonde hair with green eyes he was more of a looker, the head warrior also the Alpha's best friend but they only meet three years ago when Niko found his mate, Zoey East, in Alpha Sebastian's pack.

Niko's mate was an Omega female but don't get it twisted Omegas aren't what you hear in these bullshit stories, Omegas were like the peacekeepers they were the jokesters and they were friends with everyone.

"Yes i'm a lone wolf and i'm here to get shopping, what about you?" i ask pointing at their claws, shaking their heads they retract them in and just in time because a human lady walks by with her four kids who were bickering.

"shopping, why haven't you contacted our Alpha?" Niko asked.

"I only got here yesterday and haven't had time to find his contact, sorry i was hoping to meet someone who could give me his number" i apologize this was my act Boss told me to fit in and be this little girl who was scared of the big bad world pfft.

"It's ok, if you give us your number we'll give it to the Alpha" William says holding out his phone.

Grabbing his phone and punching my number in i thank them and say i have to go inside.

Well that went well now the Alpha has my number and i am expecting him to call tonight and the best case scenario would be that he invites me to a meeting so i can see the lay out of his land and start planning.

I had tied Cooper outside but he didn't mind he wanted a rest anyway because he was lazy, i brought a whole load of stuff mainly ingredients as i loved cooking and baking.

Once we got home i unpacked everything keeping out the things i was going to cook with, Cooper had found a comfy spot on the couch with a knit blanket watching me cook. Eating the final results was my favourite part of cooking but it was interrupted by a call.

Grinning i answer it "Hello?" i ask with my best innocent voice.

Now i had more fun with this act because it fit my appearance, i had stark white hair that fell around waist length, big blue eyes, i stood around 5'4 and i had a petite frame with long legs why do you think my parents named me Angel?

"Hi I'm Alpha Sebastian, two of my pack members say they bumped into you at the store" a deep voice came through.

Instantly i felt my knees lock up, that was sexy, such a shame.

"Oh hi Alpha, i'm so sorry i couldn't contact you before but i only moved in late last night and i couldn't find a way to contact you and i didn't want to be disrespectful coming onto pack land" i apologize profusely while rolling my eyes and smirking at Cooper.

"No it's ok you had your reasons i just wanted to ring and tell you that you're allowed in my territory and in pack land but with my beta or head warrior of course, i also wanted to invite you to a meeting so we can sign some things and get to know each other" he stated and i grin, too easy.

"Of course Alpha thank you so much it really means a lot" i say looking at my nail inside gagging, i was a little shocked as i have never had a Alpha act so friendly before.

"It's ok..." he said like he was going to say my name "I don't remember your name sorry" he sounded ashamed.

i laugh a little "It's ok Alpha i didn't give it in the first place, sorry my name is Angel Rose"

"Angel Rose that's quite a pretty name" he laughs and my eyes widen, is he flirting!

"Well i don't want to be rude Alpha but my dinner is getting cold, can we have the meeting tomorrow?" i ask hoping he says yes.

"Sure i can do that, see you tomorrow Angel" he says goodbye and hangs up.

Now don't get me wrong i have had Alpha's flirt with me before but never before they meet me, now that's new.

"Come on Cooper time for bed, i have school tomorrow" i roll my eyes and put my half eaten dinner in the fridge to eat in the morning as i really wasn't a morning person.

And like normal Cooper climbed onto my bed and cuddles up to me before we're both asleep.

Tomorrow will be interesting.

Chapter 3 ~ Questionable Meat

Waking up was a bitch i swear!

Cooper licked my arm gently and i smile "Hey buddy, you hungry?" i ask and his yips gently. Kissing his head i jump out of my warm beautiful bed and run down to the kitchen.

Pouring his food into his bowl and filling his water bowl with fresh water i ruffle his fur before getting my breakfast and heating it up.

"Argh school" i groan Boss told me that i had to go to school and involve myself with the beta and warrior to get closer to the Alpha.

Flinging my wardrobe door open i look at what to wear, now don't take the piss i may be a deadly assassin but i love clothes and looking nice, i am a girl and like to look presentable.

Putting a cute outfit together i look into my mirror, i had chosen a gray plaid skirt with thigh high socks, white converses and a plain white shirt tied into a knot at my waist.

I let my hair fall loosely down my back and didn't put any makeup on, my 'girlie' side stops at clothes unfortunately.

"Alright buddy, no chewing the furniture, the back door flap is open just don't run away because i won't chase after you and don't eat to fast" i count on my fingers at Cooper who was looking at me blankly. "Okay i might chase after you but not the point i'm off to school stay out of trouble"

Today i made sure to put my contacts in and i ran to school making it in a few minutes i walked in, everyone was staring and it was starting to piss me off. The lady at the front desk spotted me and waved me over.

"Angel Rose?" she asked and i nod smiling politely "This way" waving for me to follow her i do and she leads me to the principles office.

She knocks on the door and it opens to show a tall man with slightly grey hair and blue eyes that sparkled with wisdom and made me want to listen to all his stories, however i did notice he was a werewolf and a powerful one at that.

"Angel Rose, it's good to finally meet you" he waves me in and points to a chair opposite his desk "Now we're very excited to welcome you here, i'll just get your schedule"

He tapped a few buttons on his computer then headed to his printer, he glanced at the paper before giving it to me.

"ok so here's your schedule and as it says you have gym first period i'll provide you with a gym kit. Their very simple but then it is only gym class, could you use your shoes?" i look down at my converses and nod smiling i didn't mind at all.

i glanced at my schedule as saw he was correct i had 5 classes not including lunch

1) Gym

2) Biology

3) English

Lunch

4) Maths

5) Art

Each class was an hour including lunch the principle came over and handing me a pair of black shorts and a white t-shirt saying i could keep them.

"Now i have your locker and i would like to apologies for the number there was no other working one i could have given you, your locker number is 666 and it is just down this corridor fourth locker on the left you'll see it" he laughs "Never thought i would be giving the most unfortunate number to possibly one of the most politest kids I've met" he says shaking his head.

i laugh "Honestly, it's ok" and with that i wish him a good day and go to my first class, on the way i had a few cocky guys wolf whistle at me and a few girls give me dirty looks but i really couldn't care less.

i walked into the gym room, the whole room goes silent, i could tell some of the werewolves in here were holding back there growls at the lone wolf but there were a decent number of humans, looking around i caught the eye of Beta William and Niko as well as their mates.

Nodding my head i go towards the teacher and give him the slip the principle gave me.

"Alright kids this is Angel Rose and she is our new student, i want the uttermost respect and a warm welcome" he says slapping my back "Now go get dressed everyone we're running and playing basketball if you hurry up" as soon as he said that the werewolves run to the changing rooms but the humans huff and sulk to the changing rooms.

When i was done i walked out to see the teacher picking head captains he choose two girls one werewolf and one human and told them to pick their teams before we go running.

After a little while i saw why the humans didn't want to play basketball, the werewolf girl only picked werewolves and left the human with humans which was totally unfair it came down to the last two which was me and this huge wolf guy.

"i would like him" the wolf says smirking but that made me smirk bigger, fine they want to be unfair i'll just help the humans out, looking at my team i see a few people who i think could keep up with me and a few who didn't seem interested but they might because they are already accepting the loss that isn't coming this told me that this happens quite a lot.

"That means the new girl is with us" a guy from the human team says and i laugh giving him a hand five, some of the wolves seemed like they felt bad for what just happened but a few were smirking.

One thing my father taught me was that if you win a game or fight but it wasn't a fair one you shouldn't be celebrating but you should feel ashamed because it made you a coward.

The gym teacher gave us bibs and then told us to run four laps of the track if you couldn't do four, then two.

I started to run and noticed that some of the humans were keeping up with the wolfs making me laugh.

"What's so funny Newbie?" Niko asked smiling, i just point to the humans and speed passed him leaving him in my dust.

Four laps later and we were all getting a drink, some of the humans finished before some of the wolves making them mad.

"Okay now we'll play some basketball get in your groups and come up with a game plan" coach said and we got into our teams.

"So we're going to lose" A girl tells me keeping her eyes on the ground.

"Why?" i ask.

"They got the better players, we never even get one score" she explains.

"But now you got me, i promise we'll make scores and maybe even win" not maybe, Angel we will win.

The humans started perking up at my explanation as i told them our game plan they nod and started getting excited.

"What did you do newbie shoot them with speed?" William says looking at the human getting ready with excitement.

"No just a little encouragement, i mean humans against werewolves that's a bit unfair but now they got me so that should even things out" i laugh.

"Oh yeah! Well i wish you luck i'm a good player" he laughs and we shake hands before his mate comes over with a smile saying hi before taking William to the court.

"Okay andddd.....begin" coach says blowing the whistle, he threw the ball up and i jump smacking it back to my team mates who got the ball, the werewolves started moving in.

A were girl tried smacking the ball from a human girls hands but i step in between them and take the ball from her before she knew what happened leaving the human girl smiling and the werewolf mad.

i dribbled the ball right to their hoop and three of them started to close in but i just smile and hope they were easy to fool, without stopping i faked- pumped meaning i faked a shoot and just like i thought all three jumped up but i just moved and boom a score from the two point line.

The whistle blew again and i heard the coach shout "2-0" before we start again and it just kept going like that "4-0" "6-0" "8-0" before they got a point because one of the human boys got cocky and grabbed a were when they had the ball giving the werewolf team the ball because of a foul, i gave him a dirty look and he apologies.

"8-2" coach laughs causing a few weres to bite their lips to keep in their growls. And it wasn't long before we made it to 16-2 and won the game, the humans on my team went crazy screaming and hugging each other, they came over and lifted me up chanted and shouting in joy, i just laughed.

I noticed William, Niko and their mates laughing and clapping along with some other wolfs but most of them were mad at the fact they lost to some humans and a lone wolf.

"Nice one newbie" Niko claps "Look at lunch we have a empty seat want to take it?" he asks and i take the offer, after they leave and i went to get changed i was interrupted by a human girl "William is MINE stay away from him!" but the funny thing is it wasn't even his real mate.

"Whatever sunshine" i say walking past her but she grabbed my arm.

"He's MINE and if you try to take him i'll destroy you" she says smirking making me laugh.

"Look i don't have the time nor crayons to try to explain this to you so let me make this quick, if you do not remove my arm from your filthy paws i'll gladly break each and every finger. William is neither mine or yours, he is going out with Summer and he loves her so if you try to ruin them i'll make your life a shit show" I say this in my calmest voice and see her eyes widen as she removes her hand and moves to the side looking down.

Summer was the Williams mates name that i learned that because William wouldn't shut up about her skills in basketball that and she was on my files.

Thank the lord it was now lunch I forgot how boring school was.

"YO NEWBIE" i hear someone shout and see Niko and the group waving me over why he insisted on calling me that i had no idea but whatever. Sitting down i said hello and pulled my lunch out.

"Geez this is school Angel not a restaurant" Zoey Niko's mate laughs looking at my lunch i just shake my head smiling.

"I can't eat the questionable meat otherwise i will become paranoid" i state making Summer laugh she was so nice with her short brown hair and her big brown eyes, she was also very petite figure she stood about 5'0 and she was just so cute!

"You know girl" Zoey nods throwing her natural ginger hair over her shoulder, taking out her peanut butter and jelly sandwich making us all laugh Zoey was hella tall standing 5'9, blue eyes and she had muscles! Like if i was playing for that team gurl bye i'd have to fight Niko.

"So you ready to meet the Alpha today Newbie?" Niko asks eating a bite of the 'meat' making me shudder.

"erm sure?" i say not taking my eyes off the 'meat' then i felt something slide down my back and realize it was that human girl tipping her drink down my back.

Throwing my chair back hitting her in the process i swirl around glaring.

"Sorry" she giggles holding her hip where i hit her with my chair.

Feeling my claw come out i close my hands in fists and glare harder making her gulp.

"I'm giving you ten seconds to get out of my sight before the next thing coming out of your mouth is your teeth." i whisper and she huffs.

"I'm not scared of you!" she shouts holding her middle finger up in my face.

I grab her finger and hold it slightly bending it back i look up and see the entire lunch hall was watching.

"Now look what you've done! You have made yourself look stupid in front of all of these people" i say looking at her.

"Let go of me you slut!" she shouts in pain and i grunt letting go of her finger and sit back down.

Some of the watchers groan as the 'fight' ended but she stayed there calling me names, i was slowly losing control my wolf pushing at my control, from the corner of my eye i see William look at my eyes slightly turning black and he goes to stand up but i beat him to it.

"If i throw a stick, will you leave?" i ask innocently and she gasps.

"Who do you think you are! I'm the most popular girl here and all the guys want me not you, hoe!" she says waving her arms around to the boys who just laugh at her.

I sigh holding a hand to my nose "I thought you knew that lower prices attract more customers?" i explain like i was talking to a child.

She just screams in frustration and walks away pushing a nerd to the ground and that's when i lost control.

I jump up and ran at her full speed ready to make the kill but Niko grabs me restraining me last minute letting her run away screaming "Let go of me" i growl and i feel him shake his head.

"We actually like you Angel please don't get kicked off our territory because of some human thot" he says and i feel myself start coming back i gently remove his arms and head to the nerd who was still picking up his stuff.

i get on the floor and help him gather up all his papers and books.

"Thank you" he whispers gently.

"I'm sorry she did that because of our argument" That's one thing i hated most, innocent people getting hurt because of others, like my parents, that's why i became an assassin was to help the innocent and get rid of the guilty.

"It wasn't your fault" he looks up and smiles at me before taking his papers back thanking me again he leaves the cafeteria saying something about finding his friends, William smiles at me but then his eyes grew foggy, mind link.

"Who is she anyways?" i ask Zoey who was still eating the sandwich, when we were arguing she didn't even stop eating.

"Her names Mindy and she's irrelevant" Zoey says with her mouth full.

"Alpha says he can't do the meeting later but we can skip school and head over now" Matthew finally explains and everyone starts getting up.

"I can't skip on my first day" i say and Niko shakes his head.

"Everything will be fine the principle is the Alpha's father" he explains and i nod my head and head with them that meant the principal was the ex alpha of this pack which would explain the power sliding off of his every limb.

The walk to the pack house wasn't a long one and before you know it we were walking in to the pack area "It's just this way but he isn't ready just yet he is talking to his mother" Niko says and i nod looking around.

I felt a small hand tug at my skirt looking down i saw a small girl about four smiling up at me.

"Hi i'm Cora!" she says smiling, she was cute in a pink dress and barefoot, her black hair was in pigtails and the ends curled naturally and her big blue eyes were glistening with joy.

"Well hello Cora, i'm Angel" i say crouching down being careful about my skirt, she pulls me into a hug.

"Can you help me?" she asks and i noticed that she could speak perfectly.

"Sure how old are you Cora?" i ask and she puts five finger up i looked at her shocked.

"I know i'm a big girl!" she giggles with glee. "GIRLS!" she shouts and gets the attention of fours other little girls who looked frustrated and close to tears.

"Oh no what's wrong?" i ask heading over and a little girl in tears wraps herself up in my arms and i know you might be thinking this is weird but i have always been good with kids, people say i have a reassuring aura and it helps little ones relax as well as others who are around me.

Which always made me laugh because of my job

Rocking her i look at Cora to explain "We can't do a braid and we have been trying for hours" she whines.

"Would you like me to help?" i ask and they all nod "You ok sweetheart?" i ask the girl in my arms who had stopped crying, see i told you!

She nods and i let her go "Alright get into pairs and Cora come here please" they do as i say.

"Now grab three sections of hair" i show them and they do just as i say nodding i look back at Coras hair "Now take the left side and put it into the middle" i show them and it went like that until all of them knew how to do braids.

They were screaming in happiness and i was laughing "Can we do your hair Angel?" Cora asks innocently.

"Sure sweetie" and with that i had five pairs of hands were off to work, there was a few ouch moments but i'm an assassin i can handle a bit of hair pulling.

"ANGEL!" I hear some yell my name and see Niko coming over. "Sorry girls The Alpha wants to see Angel so i'm going to have to steal her for a little bit" the girls huff and hug me goodbye.

"Will you be back? Cora asks.

"Maybe sweetie" i say hugging her goodbye before i walk back.

"Nice hair" William says laughing and i elbow him gently pulling the braids apart.

"This way" Niko says leading me to a big door and he knocks.

"Come in" i heard the same voice i heard on the phone but in person it was much better.

The door opened and i barely made it though the door before i was pinned up against the wall.

"MATE" The Alpha growls with his face pressed into my neck.

Shit!

Chapter 4 ~ Athena

The rest of the meeting consisted in me sitting on Alpha Sebastian's lap and him asking me questions.

"I know we've only just met but i really don't feel comfortable with you living outside of the pack with the Death Assassin so close" he says holding me close to his chest.

"I'm sorry to say this but i'm not comfortable living here yet, trust me i'll be fine" i say leaving no room for arguing.

He drops his head "Fine but you put my number on your phone" that i agree to and i put my phone number into his phone and message my phone so i had his number, now you may be wondering why he didn't already have my number because he called me but it turns out he had used Williams phone.

"There" passing his phone back to him "Now Alpha I need to get home I have school tomorrow" getting off his lap I head to the door.

"You go to school with William and Niko?" He asks walking out with me.

"Yes Alpha" he growls.

"As much as I like you calling me that it's getting very hard to control my wolf Princess, so just call me Sebastian" holding my face he strokes my cheeks that had started to burn. "I'll see you tomorrow Princess" he smirks at the look of confusion on my face.

What does he mean by tomorrow? No idea as I was walking out I say goodbye to the girls who was still braiding their hair and their mothers who's give me the biggest smiles.

I don't think they'd be smiling at me if they knew what I did for a living.

The walk home wasn't long so I open my door quickly ready to see my baby.

"HEY BABY" I say in a baby voice and see Cooper getting excited jumping and barking at me "You hungry baby?' I laugh and fill up his bowl.

While I was making my dinner and lunch for school it hit me, the whole mate situation, well shit.

"Please don't go through with it" My wolf Athena, yes my wolf was named after the Goddess of wisdom not my choice but hers "Please Angel, I don't ask for much but I need him" her voice breaks.

"I know Athena, how about this I go through this like a normal mission and get to know them and when the time comes we'll know what to do" I explain to her but yes I know killing him will basically be kill us but if we don't, a lot of people will lose their lives.

"Ok Angel, I trust you. Just please don't make any quick decisions" she whispers laying down in my mind I nod and eat putting the leftovers in a container for school, I made egg fried rice with chicken breast, it was sooooo good!

I was rudely woken up at 6 AM! By Coopers big arse paws almost knocking me out, so now I have three random arse claw marks going from the corner of my eye to a little lower than my cheek bone.

"Ow Cooper! This is why mum doesn't freaking love you" I yell one of my favourite vines RIP vine, obviously without the swear word because child of God right here!

Holding my eye he whimpers hiding in his paws "Oh for gods sake Cooper mummy is only playing" I glare and he barks.

"Who do you think you're back chatting mister!" Crossing my arms I look at him with a raised eyebrow before I realised what I was doing "Oh my god I'm going crazy!"

Cooper barks as if agreeing with me but I just show him the hand "You have five more minutes before I make you food, don't be late" and with that I walk out leaving the door open because I knew if he was a kid it would piss him off.

I'm actually losing it, I'm going to be one of those crazy lady's who think their animals talk to them and don't give out sweets on Halloween like who does that!

But because I was woken up I had time to have breakfast and a cup of coffee before school...ok three cups, stop the discrimination it's 2020 gosh.

"Ok Cooper baby I'm going to school, the rules are the same no jumping the fence and running away, don't eat too fast, no chewing the furniture and stay cute" I laugh giving him a belly rub "I'll be home soon ok" kissing his head I grab my keys and go to walk out the door by Cooper barks making me turn around, there on the table was my school bag with my books and lunch.

"Oh dear, what would I do without you huh?" I give him a treat and go to the door, looking in the mirror I take one last look at my outfit.

I had chosen a simple white skirt that stopped mid thigh, a black knit cropped shirt, an oversized denim jacket and my white superstar shoes with my hair in a high pony tail and like always no makeup, I say goodbye to Cooper one last time before heading to school.

My first class was English so I put my books and lunch in my locker and made my way there, class started soon so everyone was already in there seats, walking in there was a huge growl luckily the class was full of werewolves otherwise that would be hard to explain.

Looking over at the teachers desk I was shocked at what I saw, go on I'll give you a second to guess who it was.

Place your guesses here and the winners get to give the losers a huge slap of 'I told you so' ~

~~~~~~~~

It was Alpha Sebastian! That cheeky son of a.

"Angel step outside for a second" he growls walking out and I follow him.

"Go home and get changed!" He growls looking at my outfit, his eyes turning black for a few seconds.

"No this is my outfit and I like it, end of. I didn't know when you said you'll see me tomorrow you'd get a job as my teacher but if this
~~~~~~~~

is going to cause problems Alpha, I'll see sure to it that I'll have my class changed" I say crossing my arms, he shakes his head.

"Fine but if I see one guy talk to you I'll have their heads and mark you in front of everybody" he growls stepping closer to me.

"Even in front of the humans" I whisper.

"Don't tease me Princess" he grips my arm looking at my face properly before he lets out a growl that even made me shiver a bit out of fear "who did that to you?" He says stroking my face and it clicks the marks from Cooper.

"Sebastian please, it was just my puppy calm down" I say rubbing his back as he pulled me into a hug.

"I'm sorry Princess" kissing my cheek he pulls back "Now get into class before I give you a detention" he winks slapping my arse when I walked passed.

Going back inside was so awkward because everyone got silent and was staring at me because they saw mine and Sebastian's exchange from the doors window.

From the corner of my eye I see Niko lean over "So newbie I see we have a Luna now" then he chuckles.

"White shut up and pay attention" Sebastian shouts the whole class laughs, to be fair he was a good teacher and in this class I could tell I would love coming to, one because of the hella fine man teaching it and...well that's it really.

Chapter 5 ~ Introductions

After gym Niko, William, Summer, Zoey and I head down to the lunch hall the boys went straight off to get some food while me and the girls go to their table."So Angel, how's it going with our Alpha?" Zoey winks while the boys come back."It's going" laughing at Niko when he looked at my lunch."Hey Newbie you feel up to making me lunch tomorrow?" Niko asks eyes locked on my lunch."Niko!" Zoey gasps hitting him with her elbow "Don't be rude""It's alright Zoey" I put my hand on her arm but she still glares at Niko "So how's the pack?" Asking William his smiles taking my question as me taking my Luna role but even though yes I do care because of my wolf it was really to see if I needed to step up my mission.

"Well Angel everything is ok however we have been having problems with rouges lately, it's risen dramatically but the Alpha is trying to come up with a plan" he explains.Interesting, so my mate is having a rouge problem, yes I did feel them and there has to be a whole pack full of them but I didn't see them as a threat.

However if they start putting my plan on hold I'd have to do something about them. I had opened my mouth to start eating and Niko had swung his arm out to snatch my lunch when everyone froze at a loud roar.The humans were freaking out but the werewolves knew who it came from, the all mighty Alpha.

One wolf kid stood up laughing "Yes T, you've all been pranked! We connected our phones to the schools speaker and played a wolf growl" he laughs and everyone joins in as well, he was an Omega so it seems about right.Sebastian gives him a smile in appreciation and the Omega nods his head, quick save.

Sebastian walks over taking a seat next to me "Hello Princess" he whispers in my ear making me shiver.Shaking my head I just go back to eating and Niko groans.

"No I'm hungry" Niko groans giving me puppy dog eyes I just roll mine and go to slide my lunch over to him but Sebastian's arm blocks the container."Don't even think about it" he growls lowly sliding my food back over to me and Niko go to groan again but Sebastian just glares "Don't".

"Tomorrow I want you to come in wearing clothes that cover you" He says taking a bite of my chicken closing his eyes and smirks at Niko choking on his sandwich mumbling how it wasn't fair."Let me say this once and I don't want to say it again, it is mid summer and I will not wear clothes that will cause me uncomfortable for your sanity, if you have a problem I will switch classes" my voice stern leaving to room for arguments.Sebastian just looks in the distance, stubborn Alpha.

After lunch I had Art which was one of my favourite classes, Sebastian walking next to me he leans down "Would you like a lift home today Princess?" His voice hopeful.Shrugging I allow him and tell him to meet me outside in the car park at the end of school.

Let's just say that my mate may or may not be growing on me, his silky soft black hair falling onto his olive toned skin, stormy blue eyes that was stern to most but always softened within seconds of meeting my gaze.Luscious full lips above a strong jaw even Ian Somerhalder would be jealous of, it gave him a feminine splash within the whole bad guy look that he pulled off so well.

Not to mention he was like 6'5 of pure muscle and strength, let's just say he made me look like a tiny doll next to him at my 5'4 petite figure. Pulling up to my little house I invite him in for dinner because I was a good host, Assassin or not I had manners."You live alone?" He asks looking around the quiet house."Yeah, oh and brace yourself" I say smirking just waiting for his reaction.

"Why?" I heard his voice become stiff as thought there was a problem and I see his body go to step in front of me."HEY BABY!" I scream and Sebastian looks at me in shock and anger before he heard something running this way.

Cooper comes sprinting in from the back garden to me before seeing Sebastian and try's to change direction face turning nasty to protect me."Cooper sit" I say and he freezes before sitting at my feet "oh dear, what on earth have you done?" I laugh at Coopers messy mud filled coat but he just licks my head giving Sebastian a nasty look.

"Cooper friendly" I say and he un-willingly walks over to Sebastian and I tell Sebastian to stroke him as he stood there in disbelief and amusement in his gorgeous eyes."Ok now I'm going to cook dinner if by the time I'm back you're not both friends I'll be mad" I explain sternly walking to the kitchen and they both follow.

"Do you mind me asking where your parents are?" Sebastian takes my hand as in froze."Erm, both my parents are gone" I explain voice breaking slightly.

"I'm so sorr.." he started the whole 'im sorry when did they die?' speech.

"They're not dead i know they're not, I'll give you my story another time just not today" and he nods confused but respectful taking me up in a big hug.

My wolf purrs and I felt my body relaxing."Go on a date with me, tonight" he speaks into my neck I accept his offer and we finished dinner. On the way out I fill Cooper bowls up and head out only bringing my swimwear and a towel because that all Sebastian said I would need."So we're going to a swimming pool?" Looking at my mates gorgeous face."No better, just wait and see" and then the car got silent as he drove me to our destination.

We reached a cave and I was gobsmacked, it was beautiful, inside was a natural pool made by the ocean it faced."I come here when I'm upset or when I want to be alone" Sebastian finally ends the comfortable silence we sat in.

"I can see why" still gobsmacked at the sight.

"You want to swim?" Sebastian asks even though it wasn't really a question because he stood up and started stripping, my eyes graced with the sight of his fit body, without saying anything I stood up and changed into my swim wear before jumping straight into the pool.

We had started playing about before we both were leaning up by the pools edge."You want to play 21 questions?" Sebastian asks and I nod "you start" he laughs at my sigh 21 questions wasn't my forté."How about when one person asks the question we both answer so there's no, what about you's" I explain and he nods smiling "Ok where were you originally from?""LA" "Cool I'm from Texas, your turn" I lean back into the water moving around to keep warm, Sebastian sees me shiver and hugs me under the water.

"What do you like to do when you're not working?" He speaks into my shoulder again, his warm breath giving me goosebumps."Traini ng you?" "Same" he smiles at me.

"Favourite tv show?" I grip him again because there was a breeze." The Walking Dead""Omg same!" I grin and he strokes my cheek.

"Your favourite colour Princess?" "Grey what about yours?" I ask. "hazel" and I didn't miss how he was staring into my eyes making me blush and laugh on the inside if only he saw my true eye colour.

"Cat or dogs?" I grin knowing he already knew my answer."Dogs" my body jerking with his chest as he laughs.

"Favourite food?" I feel him sniff my neck and felt his teeth graze my neck as he spoke."Pasta" I gasp and he smirks."Mines pizza, do you have any siblings?" He asks again taking my turn when he saw my blank face."No you?"

"Yeah Cora" laughing at my face "I know all she talks about is you now"

"Awww she's so cute! Alright what's your biggest pet peeve?"

"Easy, laziness yours?" "I HATE it when people eat with their mouths open" I shiver at a memory.

Fun fact this is actually my biggest pet peeve, what's yours?

"Alright my turn are you a morning person or a night owl?" Sebastian splashes my face with the cold water." Night owl duh, I'm not a morning person" I reply splashing him back."That sucks because I happen to be a very cheerful morning person" he smirks making me groan I hate morning people.

"When's your birthday Princess?" He takes my turn again thankful like I said I wasn't good at this game."November 22 making me 18, what about you old man?" I laugh making him growl.Another fun fact this is actually my birthday because I have a bad habit of forgetting their birthdays ."August 14, I'm 26 Princess why you got a problem with that?" His face dropping.

"No it's only 8 years like I've heard of worse plus we're werewolves we stop aging at 40 old man so you're lucky" just as I finish saying that he dunked me under the water making me spit out a mouthful of water when I reached the surface.

"Don't test me Princess, alright tea or coffee? Answer on the count or three, One...two..three! COFFEE""COFFEE" we yell at the same time laughing.

"What's your favourite seasonal holiday?" I shiver again.Holding me close to his chest trying to warm me up "Halloween" "Ss.s.same" teeth chattering.

I know this may be weird as werewolves have insane body temperatures but I'm only half werewolf don't forget but people just place it down to my size.

"So do you enjoy being Alpha?" He hums pulling me deeper into his chest trying to warm me up as he thinks about the question.

"I enjoy keeping my people safe, the big family vibe, being the one to help someone when they have a problem." My head rises as he takes a deep breathe "but with that level of respect comes a lot of responsibility, I knew was there but the sheer amount gave me a lot of sleepless nights".

I look up at him only just noticing the slight dark bags under his eyes, his 5 o'clock stubble.

We can help him with the stress Angel, he'll be fine. Athena sighs in pain at our mates stress.

"I will always want to put you first, always but you have to bare with me. I can't always be there to cuddle and we most likely won't be able to spend all day together most days" he sighs kissing my forehead and taking in my scent.

"But you'll always be my number 1 priority Angel" my stomach is lit with butterflies.

"When we mate I'll be Luna so I will be helping you with things, we can do this together" I didn't even notice that I said 'when' until it was too late.

"Very true my little Luna"

After we finished our questions it was past midnight "I should take you home as you do have school tomorrow and your lips have gone blue" his thumb gently tapping my bottom lip and with that he pulls us both out of the water and we both dried off.

He took me home and kissed my forehead again wishing me a goodnight, maybe this mate thing wasn't so bad, my wolf purrs in agreement.

Chapter 6 ~ Barcode

I had woken up early today and had moved to my kitchen, grabbing an apple I cut it up and go over the file again looking for something new.

I saw that Sebastian had been getting evidence that the boss had a group of assassins working for him but that's where his wrong, the boss doesn't own anyone, he might like to believe he does but he doesn't we do what we do for certain reasons; but he likes to see himself as our Alpha.

Mine was mainly for my parents but over the years I do it for all the innocent, I only really like taking missions where the person is evil. I take out a lot of rapists, killers you think of the most evil thing someone could do I've killed them.

Some assassins ask if I ever feel guilty but I don't, not the slightest which is why I'm confused as to why I'm on this mission, from the reports Sebastian is just nosey, so why would he send me on this mission?

But i'm not going to ask or he'll take me off of the mission and then Seb will die, or there's something im missing?

The boss only gives me missions like this when his desperate so Sebastian must be like a splinter under the bosses skin unwilling to let go. My wolf puffed up her chest proud of our mate but now his in trouble.

I was happy we were given this mission because if not he might have been dead already.

I came back to the real world file still in front of me whilst my right hand cupped my necklace "What do I do?" I whispered opening the locket.

My mother and father's faces looked back at me smiling holding a 6 year old me in-between them."I miss you" and with that I close the locket and head up to my room to get dressed for school.

Picking white fishnets with blue denim shorts, I wrapped a grey plaid shirt around my waist and a white cropped shirt that said suck it up on the front.

I pulled a pair of white socks over my fishnets they had a thick black band and a thinner red band above that. I threw on some normal black heeled boots over that and put my hair in two low pigtails at the nape of my neck.

I looked cute and I felt confident in my outfit, my style was one where I could have gotten my clothes from a charity shop but I worked them and I liked that.

I quickly made pancakes and put them in a container for lunch as I had already had an apple, feeding Cooper and kissing him goodbye I ran to school.

Saying good morning to the principle as I caught him going in to his office he waves with a beaming smile making me chuckle he was so cute.

I had English third period before lunch and it was quickly becoming my favourite lesson don't know why though... Finishing art I walked out picking spots of paint off my fingers, I really should start painting at home again, i forgot how freeing it was just to forget everything only focusing on your photo.

Walking into the English room I already knew what was coming and as if on cue it did, a deep growl flittered around the room causing everyone in the room to drop their eyes and made mine meet the offender.

He narrows his eyes at me but I just point at my shirt making him roll his eyes, silly Alpha male I may only be 5'4 but I'm no pushover nor shy little girl.

The lesson went fast and I had a shit ton of notes written down, I had never been good at English but I was starting to get everything, the bell went off causing all of us to wince gently from the loud shrill, we all started putting our stuff away and getting up.

"Angel please stay back for a bit" Sebastian says not even looking up at his laptop. Niko walks past me and nudges me giving me a smile.

Great just great what now.

When everyone was gone he looked up pupils dilating "What have I told you about covering up" he said in a low voice eyes raking my outfit.

I leaned on his desk palms flat "What have I told you about it being mid summer, I'm 18 Sebastian not 5. You may be my mate but you're not my father respect that! Don't forget what I told you, if this continues I will get moved from your classes. This is school not the pack house." I say his eyes go black.

"Alright I'm sorry but you have to understand I'm not doing it to be an arsehole it's just I get over protective" he closes his eyes breathing deeply walking round the desk.

He reaches over and pulls me onto his lap and I lay my head on his chest.

"I know just try to relax ok, everyone knows I'm yours alright" I whisper and he purrs at my words "Now I got pancakes want to share?" He laughs and my wolf purrs.

After school Sebastian dropped me off at my house and left apologizing saying he had a meeting which was fine because I was going out on a mission tonight anyway.

Getting into my Assassin outfit which was black leather trousers, a bullet proof vest with a black leather shirt over the top, I also have a black cloak with a hood that covered my hair.

All finished with a black mask covering everything but my eyes and knee length boots with out heels obviously.

This is why people call me the Death Assassin one because of my mark and two because you never see or hear me before its too late, some say that i actually am the grim reaper but I've met him and his a cool dude but a bit boring if i do say so myself.

A good thing about being the best Assassin was I could make my own missions and no one could say anything, well they could they just didn't want to, i just don't get paid for it but i don't care. So tonight I was going to finish this whole rouge thing.

I took comfort knowing they were all rouge and deserved it like I said before they were the lowest of the low.

Heading out it didn't take long to find a rouge on his own, so I acted fast injecting him with tranquilizer and pinning him on the floor, he passed out after a few minutes which was just pathetic, rolling my eyes I heaved him over my shoulder puffing at the sudden weight.

Taking the back roads to my house I take him straight down to my basement and chain him up to the back wall using silver.

As an Assassin we are given a rouge scanner, when the council state you a rouge you're given a bar code if you will, its a tattoo that when scanned it brings up their information, name, age, why their rouge and any family members or if you have a full name you can place that in and you get the same results.

Only Alphas are meant to have them but we got them now as well so I found his mark on his chest just over his heart where they are all placed and scanned it.

The device comes to life showing his information.

Edgar Bates, 30. Rouge at aged 21

Rouge for killing an Alpha's daughter when she refused to go out with him because he wasn't her mate and raped two other omegas causing them to have his two children, neither child has taken his name and both mothers have gone into hiding with their children changing all first and last names for their protection.

- Daughter: Ebony Swander, aged 10
- Son: Finn Jones, aged 11

My face hardens while reading his information looking up I see his face wince and he groans waking up.

"Morning Sunshine" I laugh and his eyes snap open with fear.

"Death Assassin" he whimpers as I take a step closer.

"Hello Edgar Bates" I nod as his eyes widen "No you're not my mission so you can stop pissing your pants now" his body sags against the chains causing a slight burning smell and a hiss as his skin made more contact with the silver.

"So why am I here?" he whimpers when I pull out a knife.

"Well as you asked nicely, you and your little rouge friends are targeting my mission and getting in my way" I say wiping my knife "So you will be telling me why you're targeting them and you WILL tell me where you're hiding because if not the sweet council that turned you rouge will get a little notification that you're no longer around"

That's another thing each rouge is fitted with a tracker and when a rouge is killed the council sees their tracker has gone dead so they put their files away and that's that. Many rouges try removing it but what they don't know it its attached to their hearts and the only way to remove it is to kill yourself. Tragic.

"They'll kill me" He whispered eyes wide making me laugh.

"And I won't?" I question and he starts crying. "Ok from the beginning Edgar and make it snappy, I need this over with tonight"

"Our leader wants the Alpha dead" he sniffles.

"Why Edgar come on" I bark getting mad.

"The Alpha is the reason why his a rouge and he wanted revenge" Edgar rushes out trying to please me.

"Name?" I ask and he looks at the scanner in my hand.

"Brent Parker" he whisper my ear barely catching it.

Putting the name in I was given the information.

Brent Parker, 35. Rouge at age 20

Rouge for kidnapping an Alpha's little sister and threatening to kill her if the Alpha title wasn't handed to him although he wasn't planning on giving the girl back as he had sold her to the vampires, however the Alpha had a vampire friend unbeknownst to Brent he was handing the kid to the Alpha's friend. Then attacked a council member when brought in.

Brother: Ed Parker, killed at age 30 was also rouge for helping his brother but was killed by Death Assassin, as of why still unknown.

Oh wow this was my first time seeing my name on the scanner, I thought I remembered the name thinking back I remembered why I killed Ed Parker, he was coming round the Assassin building begging for us to train him so he could get revenge but the when we refused him he killed a new assassin some little kid wasn't even 10 yet so I killed him on site without a second thought.

"So his trying to get revenge on the Alpha for making him rouge?" I question with laughter in my voice, he just nods looking at his burnt skin from the chains "Where is he?"

"About two miles north from here" He said making eye contact with me.

"How many of them is there?" I question standing up this mission was coming to an end and even he knew that due from the knowing look in his eyes he wasn't ready to go but he'd rather go by me then some ratty rouge.

"20 give or take they are mainly on guard and there's three guys around Brent like body guards but their nothing special, it might be easier to go by trees if you can and theirs a witch coming to the area in about three hours to help Brent with scent changes and she was going to try stop the tracker" Edgar says still not removing his eyes from mine.

"I know what I have done is wrong and I deserve everything you do right now but please believe me I didn't want to do this, he said he knew where my kids were and he would kill them if I didn't help him, it may not seem it but I loved the two girls it talks about in my information, I didn't rape them I swear they were on their heat and we just couldn't help it I wish it never happened but I love my kids so when he said that I panicked" he explained.

It made sense.

Both girls went into heat and at the two times it happened he was dating the females so it seemed natural for both girls and him unfortunately then his wolf was getting mad because he had two kids and no mate and wanted to mate the alphas daughter but she refused and his wolf retaliated.

"Your kids will be safe after tonight I will find them and make their mothers move again along with changing their names just in case he told anyone their whereabouts" I say writing a note on the side so I didn't forget.

"Thank you, I know you're going to kill me but I'm thankful, you're going to save a lot of lives tonight" he closes his eyes "Please do it now" he whispers.]

I pulled out my knife "I'm sorry your wolf got the better of you" I say and a tear escapes from his eyes.

"Never again" he laughs and with that I drive my knife in the side of his head making it a quick easy death, damn that was the first kill I've done where I felt bad maybe the mate bond was making me soft!

"You know that's not true" Athena laughs feeling slight sorrow for the man in front of us "Now stop whining and do your mark we've got a lot of work to do"

Stepping forward I place my hand on his forehead smelling burning skin was never a fun moment but it had to be done.

Stepping back I looked at the DA burn of his forehead and unchain him catching his dead body before it hits the ground, calling the boss I tell him my mission and he says he'll have helps come after to clean up after me, he also said to knock out the witch so he can investigate her which was odd because we never leave behind people but whatever.

Walking out I head north taking his advice going by the trees, it didn't take long before I saw the tents set up and just like he said almost every rouge was on look out and there like he was the fucking king sat Brent Parker with three rouges around him lowly speaking to each other.

There were about 20 rouges walking around well this is gonna be fun.

"Why hello Death Assassin" Brent called out making me smirk "What you might not know is I'm very good friends with a witch and she showed me this happening"

Rolling my eyes I jump down from the tree I was in and all of the rouges took two massive steps back fear stinking up the area and it sure wasn't mine.

"Oh stop being pussies! There's 20 against 1" Brent shouts but no one takes their eyes off of me.

"Such a shame that a lot of people have to die tonight, when you could have just minded your own god damn business and stayed out of this" I say calmly at everyone.

"Why you so mad Death Assassin, how about you mind you're business" Brent shouts face going red.

"I would have but you're getting in the way of my mission" I laugh making eye contact with him, he gulped before his eyes lit up with excitement.

"You're here to kill Sebastian?" he questions and my wolf growls in my head at the rouge.

"That's none of your business now you all have to die" I chuckle.

"No one is dying tonight but you, my witch told me so herself" Brent waves me off and making me snort at his statement.

"That's funny because my very own witch told me I'm not going to be killed by some pathetic Rouge" I laugh and Brent growls lunging at me but I just throw him off.

Putting a wall of fire around all of us so no one could run off I started killing each and everyone of them.

Some tried facing the fire but as soon as they touched it they were ash in seconds.

A little while later I heard a gun shot and felt a burn in my shoulder, while I may not be effected by silver like most werewolves it still burned like a bitch.

Reaching back I wiggled the bullet out before launching it into a rouges head, dead.

That's when shit got crazy people were freaking out because if that was any normal werewolf I'd be on the floor screaming out in pain but here I was pulling out the bullet and fighting back.

People were throwing themselves at the fire for a quick death while others were throwing themselves at me praying one would end me but it never happened.

Sure I got a good couple of cuts and bruises but nothing serious at all and not long after it was just me and Brent.

"Wow looks like you need a new witch" I laugh at his face, growling he lunges at me but I swipe my claws a crossed his face making him roar in pain and anger.

He shifted into his wolf and I stayed in my half changed state, running at me full speed I wait until he lunges at me again before throwing myself under him and throwing my sword through his chest.

his body landed on top of me still wheezing throwing him off he shifted back and looked at me, his life slipping from his eyes.

"Ed" He whispered with his last breath before his heard finally gave up.

Ripping my sword out and cleaning it on my leg before upholstering it back on my back.

"Now to get you back to Sebastian" I say to myself looking at his body.

I tried lifting him but my shoulder still hadn't healed and it wouldn't for the next couple of days so I winced at what I had to do.

Burning my mark on his forehead I take my sword back out and swing down removing the head from the shoulders.

I close my eyes and counted to ten trying not to heave before putting it in a bag I turn around and drop the wall and place my mark on everyone who wasn't ash.

At my house I had noticed Edgar's body was gone and everything was cleaned up nodding at the sight I head upstairs to shower.

After I patched up my shoulder and went around my house with a scent changer to get rid of any rouge scent in or around my house as well as on me.

Walking in I saw Cooper staring at 'the bag' on the counter "Upstairs Cooper" I say and he go licking my hand on the way.

Now for the next part of the plan, I got the paper out a wrote a note.

Hello Alpha Sebastian,

I have been watching your pack and I have seen your small rouge problem so I have decided to take care of it. No need to thank me I did this from the kindness of my heart, even if you do not believe it. Their presents was annoying me and distracting me from my mission and we can't have that alpha can we?

Now you may be wondering why I'm in your wonderful area? But trust me all will be revealed soon and my main reason for this letter is to show you I'm not going to hurt you and you can trust me. I have been close enough to have killed you and your pack many times but I'm hoping I don't have to hurt anyone in your pack as it won't help anyone or have any good outcomes.

However if you carry on looking for me and trying to kill me I will be forced to teach you a lesson. Now I know my reputation is harsh and believe me everything you heard was true but just trust me with this I will not harm you or your pack if anything think of me as you very own bodyguard clique isn't it? But I also wanted to tell you no matter how hard you try you will not be able to find any real facts about me as your the only person that will survive any contact with the Death Assassin and not be killed. Just know this 1) I will not harm you or your pack including any of their human friends, I give you my word 2) If you have a problem just send me a letter to the address that sent this to you but trust me even if you wait there you won't catch me.

3) Don't worry about your mate Alpha, I give you my word I will not touch her because I have no interests in hurting her and I promise no one else will hurt her. 4) However that being said, cross me and I know she doesn't live with you and she lives by herself an easy kill if I do say so myself so I'd advise other wise.

Enjoy now not having to deal with the rouges and now knowing you don't have to worry about me however, I would like to make a simple request. Do not tell anyone other then the ones you trust with your life because if this gets out to the people who asked me to kill you which is true I was sent to kill both you and your pack but I have my own ideas and beliefs, but if you tell someone and it gets out I will be forced to kill you all, which I really don't want to do so ensure whoever you tell won't blabber.

Death Assassin.

And with that I put 'the bag' into a box and placed the note in the box and sent it to Sebastian's office directly.

Chapter 7 ~ Stupid Boy

Walking in to school the next day i could already tell something bad was going to happen, i had dressed in a cute white and grey romper with a fedora hat and my hair in a messy fishtail braid on one side plus my white converses like normal, i felt cute and i walking in with my head high.

Having English i walked in smiling excited to see my mate again but he just looked at me and just had to open his stupid mouth.

"This is school Miss Rose, not a photo shoot" a few girls laughed but my new group didn't find it funny they all sat there in shock that what he said came out with such disgust.

Feeling tears come to my eyes i shook my head and stood up throwing him a dirty look, realising what he had done he stepped forward but i just threw hand up and carried on walking out.

Idiot! Stupid mate!

'He didn't mean it Angel' Athena whimpers

'Doesn't mean he can say it though' she nod agreeing with me.

"Angel!" he calls out trying to stop me but i ignore his calls and carry on walking not knowing where i'm going, i'm not surprised thought when find myself on the PE track.

Seeing the Coach i go over "Hey Coach, can i just run the track down please?"

"Sure Angel just don't be out here for too long it looks like it might rain soon" nodding he takes his class in to play dodge ball i think.

And with that i ran, i ran all the angry out.

Did my stupid mate not know who I was? I was the most feared assassin in the world, no one knew what I looked like because no lived to tell the tale and yet here he was telling me what to wear.

I heard the lunch bell ring, fuck i've been running for three hours.

Not being bothered to face the rest of the day i went to the shops to finish my weekly shop then went home to my baby. Just as i was about to eat dinner and enjoy a glass of wine there was a knock at the door and it just screamed stupid.

Rolling my eyes i walk over and open the door not even looking at him i just turn away and walk to the kitchen but not long after i head the door close and heavy footsteps coming closer.

Dishing a stupid plate i set it down and began eating in the stupid silence, gulping some well deserved glass of wine, a feeling bubbled up in my stomach.

"How did you get wine?" and with that i erupted into laughter.

Ten minutes later we were both started to calm down.

"i'm sorry Angel, i shouldn't have done that" he whispers pulling me closer.

"I'm sorry too" i say and he looks at me confused "i called you stupid in my head a lot" i giggle and he laughs.

"Oh princess" he chuckles.

"But i want to get this clear, if anything like that happens again i will get my classes changed, this is school not the pack house" i raise my eyebrows and he holds up his hands.

"Fine but we eat now the food will get cold and i have something to show you".

After dinner he pulls out a familiar piece of paper and my heart races a little, but then i blush remembering that i told him to only tell the people he trusted with his life, i didn't think he would show me.

"I can't believe it, we have been planning to kill them for months now and the Death Assassin comes in and kills them in one night? Damn. I told the pack about the rouges but told them we were stopping the man hunt on the Death Assassin, i told them we needed to get back to full strength. But i feel a lot better now with the Death Assassin being on our side"

"Who else knows?" i ask genuinely curious but happy he choose to tell me.

"Just William, Niko and their mates"

"Do you think the Death Assassin will stay true to their word?" i ask him reading the note again.

"For some reason i feel like i can trust the note" he whispers like i'll find him stupid but i just nod and we eat dinner.

"You're a good cook" he says with a full mouth i laugh and throw him a napkin when a bit fulls out.

"Thanks, i guess when you're on your own for a long time you have a lot of free time on your hands and i was fed up with eating pot noodles and beans on toast so i brought a cook book and taught my self" shrugging and finishing my wine.

"well you're good, maybe you can teach me some time" he laughs cleaning the table.

"Maybe" i smile and we head to the living room.

Sitting on his lap with my head on his chest i felt myself starting to fall asleep, his hand was running through my hair making my wolf purr.

"Come on Princess, let's get you to bed" he whispers cradling me to his chest and he started walking up the stairs, Cooper leading the way knowing it was bed time.

he gently placed me on the bed "Does he sleep with you?" he asks raising one of his eyebrows.

As if answering his question Cooper snuggles into me and i start falling asleep.

"I'm sorry about today Princess" And with that he kissed my forehead and went home but i was too out of it to say anything, but i did know i didn't have any lunch for school tomorrow.

Chapter 8 ~ Scary Movies

I started my day in a bad mood and the fact that i was running late was not helping my mood, i not only forgot to make lunch yesterday but i also had forgotten to set my alarm so i woke up at 8.

School started at 8:30, throwing my sheets off of me i growled "Fuck! That boy is throwing me off"

'Don't start blaming our mate Angel' Athena growls.

"Not today Athena, i'm not in the mood" Growling again i stomp to my wardrobe and pull on some grey tracksuit bottoms with a cropped shirt and my boots.

Running a brush through my hair i ran downstairs filling Coopers bowls up.

"I love you baby, i'll be back soon" With that i was out the door running to school, The run wasn't long but it had started raining which worsened my mood even further.

"Well if it isn't my beautiful mate" Sebastian smiles at me at the door of my English class but i just walk in ignoring him as a punishment for making me late.

"Ok then? Today class we're looking at Shakespeare" His eyes never once leaving me, i felt bad sure but he made me late and now i'll have to eat the bad food here and probably die!

My classes didn't drag out too long which was good but my mood hadn't gotten any better through out the day but thankfully it was lunch now which brightened my mood slightly. The guys had been trying to help me all day but it was no use.

Sitting at our lunch table i looked down in glum.

"Alright enough of all of this baby stuff, what's wrong and you will tell me otherwise i will force you to eat this bad school food that you hate so much." Niko says holding up his fork which had meat juice falling through the holes of the fork making even him wince.

"Fine! Ever since i came here my head has been all over the shot, i can't do anything right! I'm waking up late, forgetting to do things, putting important things to the side all for one person and i'm not used to that" i say but to the end i whisper realising why i was upset.

Soon i would have Boss on my back about how this mission is going and i think i'm falling in love with the person i'm meant to kill.

"It's the mate bond Angel, everything will work out and be fine, you're a smart girl whatever you need to do you'll figure it out" Summer says not even looking up from her book.

Everyone looks at her weirdly but my eyebrows shoot up, did she know what i was here do to?

My train of thought was ruined by someone placing a chicken sandwich in front of my face with fresh orange juice and a cookie, looking up i see my mate staring down at me.

"I remembered you didn't make lunch yesterday and you don't like their food so i make sure to pack extra" Sebastian said sitting next to me.

"Uh oh" William whispered making us all look up "The feeding stage! It's the worst he will become insinuated with feeding you" Everyone laughed apart from Sebastian.

"It's already started hasn't it?" William stated and Sebastian nodding blushing.

"What is he going on about?" i asked Sebastian.

"When an Alpha or Beta meets their mate they go through stages of the mating bond but one of the worst ones is the feeding stage, we have this burning desire to feed our mate to make sure their well looked after and it might sound cute but it gets out of hand if you don't have food in your hand we panic because it means we're not looking after you and our wolves feel like your starving even though you may have just eaten" he explains unwrapping the sandwich but then stopping himself.

"So you will be getting me food all the time?" i question taking a bite but he just nods watching me intently as i ate "Good that means i can sleep in instead of cooking" i smirk and he laughs hugging me.

"I'm glad your happy now, As i was going to say earlier will you come stay at the pack house tomorrow as it's the weekend?"

"i can't what about Cooper?"

"Bring him plus Cora wants to see you again" He winked holding my sandwich up for me to eat which i did.

"Fine i'll go home with you if you take me back for Cooper and my things" he nods and that's what we did.

After my last lesson i met Sebastian outside in the car park and we drove to my house in a comforting silence.

Getting to my house we walked in and get bombarded by Cooper. "Come on baby, we're going for a trip" I stroke his head and he runs and grabs his favourite toy before sitting at the door while wagging his tail "Smart boy".

I throw together a bag with two outfits and any toiletries before running back down to see Cooper jumping up on Sebastian.

"Ready?" he smiles gently pushing Cooper down but still petting him. nodding we go to his car, Cooper gets in the back and lays down with his toy.

"Angel!" a bunch of young start screaming and running over to say hello.

" hello cuties" I smile and hug them all.

"Cora said you taught her how to braid hair, can you teach us?" a cute little girl with ginger hair asked.

"Sure sweetie" and that's how I spent the next two hours was teaching the young girls how to braid and even a few teenagers came over.

"Hey Newbie can we steal you back now?" Niko came over with the group and they were smirking.

"It's ok sweetie its past their bed time anyway" one of the mums said when I looked back at the kids.

"Oh I'm sorry" I apologise feeling bad.

"Don't apologise you saved me a job, she has been going on about meeting you to teach her all week" the mother laughs and the kids hug me goodnight.

"Right lets go watch a film" Niko claps his hands together walking off and we all follow. The boys ended up picking a horror which I didn't mind but half way through I saw Summer keep jerking and her eyes filling up with tears.

"Alright that's enough of that" I say getting up to turn off the telly.

"Why you scared?" Niko laughs and I turn seeing Summer look down.

"Theres nothing wrong with being scared, fear is a natural human feeling and if you don't get scared you need help, some people find horrors scary. I mean they are made to scare you so if you want to be some hard nut go for it" I say pausing the telly and sit next to Summer.

"Oh Summers scared?" Niko questions "Humans do get scared easy though"

Jumping up I storm over and get in his face "Anything wrong with that?" from the corner of my eye I see Zoey stand up which is understandable mates are everything, your bestfriend of years could have a fight and you'll still kill them for your mate.

Sebastian stands up and growls at Zoey which makes Niko growl but I snap my fingers in his face "Well? Do you have a problem that Summer is a human?"

He breathes deep and his wolf comes out "Of course not! My human was joking and I'm sorry if we upset you Summer and Luna, my Human was embarrassed because the film was scaring him and he didn't want to admit it"

I smirk " thank you" he nods and draws back Nikos face reddens.

"I'm sorry Summer" he says looking at her.

"Its ok Niko, I didn't take offense" she laughs "Maybe we can watch a comedy instead?" she asks and everyone laughs.

"Dang you're cute when your mad" Sebastian pulls me into his lap.

"Yeah? Well I'm going to get real fucking adorable if you carry on" I say jabbing him in the stomach "Now I'm hungry, coming to help?" he nods and stands up carrying me to the kitchen.

"I can walk you know" I laugh and wiggle to get down but he grips tight.

"I know but you're mine and I will carry you around, now what do you want me to do?"

"Just chop the veggies please" he salutes me then gets knife and starts cutting.

We had a few minutes silence before Sebastian swears loudly and hisses "What?" I ask whipping round and running over to him.

"It's ok I just cut my finger" he smiles.

"No come on werewolf or not, Summer would you mind finishing off dinner?" I ask and she nods.

After dinner that Summer had finished we all got ready for bed, "Goodnight everyone" I say and head into the room.

Jumping on the bed it was so comfy, sighing I just sink in deeper to the sheets.

"Move aside beautiful" Seb smiles by the door but just before he got the chance Cooper was up in his space getting comfy like he normally does beside me.

A deep growl erupts from across the room and I look up to see Sebs eyes turning black and his canines coming out.

Cooper just looks up and growls back not moving a muscle "He doesn't like to share" I laugh and Seb growls back.

"Cooper shush" I hush him and he moves to the end of the bed. Seb gets in muttering about the dog.

"Are you getting jealous of a puppy?" I laugh my eyes fluttering closed. "Seb?" I whisper falling asleep.

"Yes princess?"

"I need to tell you some things tomorrow" and with that I passed out.

In the morning everyone was still asleep so I made breakfast with the cooks for the whole pack and after about three hours of working everyone started to get up.

"Luna the Alpha has called for a pack meeting including you" one of the cooks said.

"What could he possibly want?" I laugh and head out with everyone else, Seb was standing on a makeshift stage facing a huge crowd and in that moment my Assassin instincts kicked in, he found out and now his going to kill me in front of his whole pack.

"Hello everyone, you must all know why I called you together" Seb says his Alpha voice coming through, everyone turns and looks at me.

This was worse than I thought, they already know.

"shut up Angel" Athena laughs.

"This stunning girl before you is my mate, and therefore your Luna, we won't be having the mating ceremony yet as the ex Alpha and Luna aren't here right now but they'll be back soon. However I still wanted to introduce you to her, Angel come join me" He smiles holding out his hand.

Oh god! Walking forward I take his hand.

"In a few weeks time this beautiful girl will be your new Luna I expect you all to respect her".

Walking inside I grab Seb and take him to his room.

"You should know about my past so I am going to tell you" I make him sit down "I was 6 and it was bedtime, my mother was reading me a story. We had the same hair but she always wore it up in a bun but I remember her being beautiful, my father had already said goodnight and had given me a kiss. his eyes were shining with love when he walked out, we had the same eyes as well."

seb kissed my hand ushering me to continue.

"He had gone downstairs to tidy up, it wasn't long before I was falling asleep but I was jerked awake by my fathers screams of pain, it was horrible, haunting I still remember their screams" I sniff and seb hugs me close.

"My mother placed me in our hideout, gave me my necklace and told me not to come out no matter what I heard, she shut the door and not long after her screams joined my fathers, someone came into the room looking for me but they couldn't find the room. After what seemed like hours i left the hideout but i couldnt find them" Seb pulls me close wiping my eyes dry.

"i think they're alive and I've been looking for them ever since" i look up into his eyes.

"We'll find them Angel, me and you, together. We'll find them i promise".

"Can we nap?" I sniff and he nods laying down holding me close.

And with that I feel asleep in his arms. I know I didn't tell him the whole stories but I didn't want to open up completely yet.

Chapter 9 ~ Trap?

Waking up to a message from boss wasn't the best way to start the day.

Death Assassin,

You have a day mission. I have been missing some money from a client, he is a vampire and he rapes and kills all his victims.

I will message you his whereabouts, just dispose of him and get back to your mission.

Boss.

So professional I roll my eyes deleting the text.

"Hey baby" I jerk and remember I was in bed with Seb, that was so close.

"Hey, erm i'm going to go furniture shopping today" I state sitting up

"Okay if you just give me ten minutes we can go" He yawns sitting up.

"No I kind of wanted to go alone just because I just have a lot to think about" I explain to him feeling slightly guilty about lying to him.

"Oh no, that's ok sorry"

Heading off I look at the directions I was given by the Boss leading me to a small run down building of flats I shudder and walk up the stairs.

Walking into the small flat, I just walk right and was confronted with three young girls tied up and gagged kneeling behind the dead body of my mission. Well this is interesting as I move forward to untie them their eyes widen and the one in the middle screamed.

Spinning round I dodge the knife aimed at my neck by a hair.

"Well if it isn't the little Death Assassin" Before me stood three boys, two looked nervous and the shortest one looked furious.

"You didn't tell us it was her! What the fuck man she'll kill us" one of the boys shout turning to the short one who was clearly the leader and he winces.

"Don't be stupid she's just a girl" the leader shouts raising his knife.

"No you're just new, she's been the best assassin for years you fucking idiot, we're sorry Death Assassin we didn't know it was you he said this was a mission, we don't want any trouble" the other one says hands up he bows slightly.

"Whatever just leave" I order.

"I ain't scared of you little girl" he sneers.

"Leave now and you won't be hurt" I say calmly my eyes hardening, the two taller boys bow slightly and run out."Pussies, well what's the quote everyone says? If you want something done right you have to do it yourself? Yeah something like that" and with the end of his sentence he lunges for me.

Barely missing the knife again I slam my fist into his chest sending him back a good few feet, bring my hands up I grin."Bring it bitch"

He launches himself towards me but I just dodge and roll off to the side, standing up he was already in front of me swinging.

His hands were flying everywhere and he was very un-coordinated but he had a knife and that made him dangerous.

I punch him in the stomach making him wheeze and bend over but he recovered faster than I had expected, swinging his arm up he caught me with his knife.

A long slash across my cheek, hissing I kick him away while swiping my fingers across my cheek, My hand comes back red from blood.

My eyes flashed amber as my wolf started to come to the surface. Seeing this his eyes widen in fear and he lunges for the girls grabbing the one in the middle.

But what he didn't see was my hand reaching for one of my knives. "Get on the ground and no one gets hurt" he says sweat and blood dripping from the top of his nose.

Bending my knees he sees I'm going down and relaxes his arm slightly, that's all I needed.

Flinging my arm forwards I let go of my knife and it hits its target, his dead body hits the ground with a thud and the girls whimper.

Going over I untie them all, "listen, I'm sorry you got pulled into that but I can swear to you, you are all safe now" they nod and take a seat while I call the Boss.

"Boss speaking..." his cold voice seeps through the phone.

"It's Angel, I went to my mission only for it to be a trap. A guy had recruited two assassins to kill me saying it was a mission" I lead off into silence.

He stutters "n..no it wasn't! I wouldn't have called for your de..de ath"

Rolling my eyes "Of course Luca I was just letting you know"

"Well I deeply apologise, I will be sending you double for the inconvenience" he clears his throat "is that all?"

"Yes sir" and with that I hang up, shortly after I get a notification that the money has been transferred.

Walking over to the girls I sat down facing them "I understand that this is all confusing, but it's against the law for you to know about my kind as your humans"

Their eyes widen and one of them starts crying "I promise I won't say anything! I don't want to die" she whimpers.

"I never said anything about you dying? I have a pill for you to take, I will be taking you to a hotel you just have to take the pill" I explain "what it does is it erases your memories of tonight, you'll be confused but you won't remember anything"

They start thanking me "No worries, right let's go"

Getting in a car from the Boss I take them to a nearby hotel and pay for their rooms, walking the girls to their rooms I watched them take the drug and be knocked unconscious, they knew this would happen is it was a side effect.

Knowing that all three girls were out cold I left and walk down to the receptionist who just so happened to be a wolf thankfully.

I explained to her that they had seen someone shift and they had been given the drug just to say they walked in intoxicated.

Heading back to my house I saw Sebastian waiting at my door, shit.

"Hey princ..." his greeting was cut short when he saw my face growling he grabs me and shoves me into his chest.

"Who" he growled out through his teeth, his eyes were almost fully Amber which was a bad sign.

"Please calm down, it was these two human boys trying to rob me, I'm ok"

"Why didn't you call me?"

"I didn't want to worry you" I say running my nails gently over his arm causing goosebumps to appear. "Let's go inside ok?"

With that we head in side and go straight to bed, we ending up watching telly for the rest of the night, not that I minded but he growled at any noise pulling me closer.

Waking up in my mates arms wasn't as terrible as I made out, Athena was purring, poking him he opens his eyes and smiles.

"Yes princess?" His morning voice was gruff and I felt butterflies awaken in my tummy.

"Er...erm..I" shaking my head to clear my thoughts I look up at Seb "I need a shower can you let go please"

He chuckles and lets go throwing his arm over his eyes.

"Are you still going for that shower or do you wanna carry on with our cuddle?" He lifts his arm looking at me with amusement when I didn't move.

Blushing I ran from the room, his laugh following me.

Stupid mate pull.

After my shower I realised I hadn't brought any clothes in with me so I tightened my grip on my towel and walked into my room but my bed was empty and made.

Slightly panicking I look around only to find Seb in my wardrobe.

"Can I ask what your doing?" I clear my throat.

He yells in fear as I scared him " I'm picking out your outfit today My love"

I was going to argue but his pet name for me melted my heart so I just sat down and waited.

Turning round he saw me and his eyes instantly went black with lust.

"Alright Romeo out you go" I usher him out the room and turn back to his outfit.

Rolling my eyes I saw he had picked a pair of white jeans, a grey Adidas jumper with white writing, my white superstars and a grey ankle socks.

It was actually a cute outfit so I wore it just to shut him up. Walking down the stairs into the kitchen he growls "WHAT NOW?" I laugh.

He mutters "it's unfair no matter how much skin you show the guys won't keep their eyes off you" I blush and tell him to shut up, when we had eaten we were off to school.

Fun.

Chapter 10 ~ Pleasure

School was an absolute drag, nothing exciting happened but I got to pretty much spend the day with my mate so I'm not complaining.

At lunch I decided to spend it with Sebastian in his classroom, when I walked in he was on the phone.

"Yes of course Oliver, i'll come down and see you soon, alright bye" He hung up and put his phone down, turning round he saw me at the door "Well hello beautiful".

"Good afternoon, who was that?" I ask falling into a chair in front of him.

"That princess was my friend Oliver and the leader of the vampires" and with he pulled me into his lap and took a bite from his lunch, while I sat there shocked.Most vampires and werewolves stay apart however there was no war between us anymore.

"You're going over there?" I ask turning to look at him.

"We're going, that is if you want to come" he looks at me in question.

"I don't know, I've never met a vampire before" which wasn't really a lie, sure I've killed vampire but never met them.

"Hey it's ok, they won't hurt you. I'll be there the whole time" he gentle pushes some hair out of my face and kisses my forehead.

"Mhh ...o.okay" whispering as I lean into his kiss, it felt so safe."You can leave Cooper with my pack I promise he'll be safe while we're gone, and we'll be driving. It's a long drive so dress comfortable ok?" His head was pressed up to my neck and he sniffed me "I'll come pick you up after you pack ok baby girl?"

"Ok Seb, how long will we be there for?""No longer then a week".

Once I made it home I started packing my bags for a week and I had a few weapons on me as well just in case, I also packed a bag of Coopers food and a few toys for him.

"Hey princess you ready?" A voice behinds me questions, I scream and turn around ready to fight."Woah! Hey it's ok! It's just me!" Sebastian shouts holding his hands up in a surrender hold.

"How did you get in here?" Taking my hand off the silver knife in my bag.He smile sheepishly and holds up a key.

"You got a cut out of my house key?" I shout in disbelief.

"Erm..no, well I mean yes but it's not as bad as it seems... I mean it is but I'm your mate...it's still creepy isn't it?" Hanging his head in shame he looks at the floor "I'm sorry, I just thought it would be ok, I made you one for the pack house too" he holds out a key.

"How?" I take the key."How what?" He asks bringing his head up looking at me in confusion."How did you do it?" I narrow my eyes in suspicion.Rubbing his neck in embarrassment his cheeks take a rosy appearance "ohh that, well I may or may not have got a press when you were sleeping"

"What the fuck Seb! You can't do that!" I step back what else has he done whilst I was sleeping."I know I'm sorry it's just you live here alone and I'm worried about you" he steps forward but I just take a step back and he winces.

"What else have you done while I'm sleeping?" I glare at him."Not hing! I swear just that, I'm so sorry. I definitely overstepped" "Yes you did now please give me the key" I hold my hand out."I'm so sorry I really didn't mean for it to come off as creepy" his eyes take a sheen to them as he places the key in my hand, I give him his one back but he just shakes his head.

"Please keep it" he takes another step forward and I stay where I am, seeing me do this he takes a few more before his right in front of me.

"I'm sorry" he mutters again holding out his hand.Sighing I step forward and hug him "stop apologising, I get it. It's not ok but I understand" He nods looking down like a puppy who just got put into time out "now let's get a move on".

He takes my bags and take them to his car whilst I look at his key, his crazy but my wolf couldn't stop purring at the fact he was worried for us.

Once we dropped Cooper at the pack house we set off, turns out it's an eight hour drive. Sebastian had told niko and William to take their mates in one car whilst we take the bags.

After two hours I already needed to pee so we stopped at a gas station and all three of us girls ran in to use the bathroom, finishing up we then almost brought the whole shop with everything yummy for the trip.

Seb laughed and stole a mars bar off of Me making me growl, "Keep your dirty hands to yourself" I growl but he just winks placing a hand on my thigh.

We feel into a comfy silence but I bent over and turned on the radio.

Post Malone's song better now came on and i whooped and started singing to it, Seb laughed and joined in causing me to pause.

An hour later we were joking around and laughing when I decided I was going to ask asked he knew and was friends with a vampire."So how comes you know this vampire?"

He pauses knuckles turning white on the steering wheel "Before I became the Alpha I guess you can say I was a party animal, I loved the environment but one time I got cornered by a group of new turns"

New turns were newly turned vampires and were blood thirsty, normally their creator will keep them locked up and fully fed with donated blood but some vampires are arseholes and will just turn people for the sake of it. Meaning they're alone for the turning and everything but there is a main clan that keep eyes and ears out for newly turns and will take them and look after them.

"I got cornered by them and the clan had already heard of them so they followed the breadcrumbs and found me with them" he smiled like he was reliving a memory."Oliver is the leader of the clan and we became friends because he saw that I didn't straight out kill them as most werewolves would"

I nod understanding that.

"His also helped me out in the past and I'll forever be grateful for him" his hands tighten on the wheel again and I decide to leave it there for now.

Taking a nap I didn't think I'd sleep for long but when i woke up i was in a bed, walking out of the room I started to follow the noisy voices coming to a kitchen I walk inside and there sat around a table was my group and some vampires.

Seb comes over, hugging me he takes me over to his chair and I just sat in his lap.

"Princess this is Oliver, Oliver this is Angel my mate"

I look up and catch eyes with a tall ginger man, his red eyes narrow slightly before his faces goes flat.

"Pleasure"

Chapter 11 ~ Good Girl

We had been at this vampire den for a few days now and my suspicion was growing.

Sebastian had been signing peace agreements when he told me the rest of his story with Oliver.

"A rouge had heard I was going to take over and he thought I'd be a easy target so he said I had to pass over my Alpha rights or he'd kill me" Sen snorted "So I told him to piss off, however he wouldn't take no for an answer so about a month later he saw some pups playing by the woods and Cora was there"

His hands tightened on the desk leaning forward " he took her, Cora." Growling he let go and pulled me into his lap like something was going to snatch me up "he sent me a letter saying he was going to kill her if I didn't give him the Alpha title, so I agreed. But after I agreed he handed Cora to vampire so they'd kill her"

I gently run my hands through his hair willing him to continue "Luckily he gave her to Oliver, Oliver contacted me telling me he had

Cora and he'd keep her safe and with him until he was gone, so I caught him and took him to the council to give him his punishment"

He growled again "But they didn't sentence him to death, just to be a rouge. It was him and his brother and they were planning revenge but his brother was killed by the Death Assassin and then he followed the same fate"

"It's ok Seb, they're gone now and Cora is safe" I gently calm him.

"I know Princess, I'm really sorry but I have to go to a meeting with another Vampire leader. I'll be back soon ok?"

"Ok Sebastian, I'll see you later" He gently kisses my forehead, lifting me he places me back into the chair and leaves.

I just sit there for a few minutes trying to take in all that information when Oliver walked in."Finally you're alone'

I raise an eyebrow and he stands leaning over me.

"I know who you are, Death Assassin" he snorts leaning closer and his vangs slowly drop down but I just sit there calmly.

I had figured he knew after the first day but I wasn't sure how he found out.

"Let me make this clear Angel, if you hurt Sebastian in anyway even if it's just a single hair on his head. I'll kill you, even if I die trying" he hisses at my name slightly.

I push him away from me but stay seated "I'm not planning on killing him, I have grown quite fond of my mate Oliver, however I'm sure you know how I work? I was indeed sent here to kill him" He hisses, eyes flashing "why?"

"I got the notification about a month ago, his been getting to close to my boss. My boss doesn't like nosey people so he sent me to get rid of the problem, the only worrying thing is I have a month left before he sends someone else" "Fuck! Look I won't tell him because you need to find out by yourself, just trust Sebastian. Everything will make sense in the end"

"What?" I question."Shut up his coming" he hisses and retracts his vangs.

Sebastian walks in confused "Oliver no one was there?" "Oh? Maybe they decided not to come but I just got some information from one of my clan members, that guy you're looking into has caught wind of you and has sent Death Assassin after you"

My eyes bulge out of my head and I choke on nothing, what is he doing!"How do you know that?" Sebastian steps closer to me rubbing my back trying to comfort me.

"They caught a Assassin and they told us man you need to be careful" Oliver steps forward.

"Man I completely forgot to tell you, you know those rouges?" He asks "Fondly" Oliver answers sarcastically.

"Well we had been planning for a month to try and end them but one morning I get a box sent to my office and it stunk of blood and rouge so I opened it and found his head Oliver with a burnt DA on his forehead and a letter" he laughs "basically the letter was from the Death Assassin saying that they was sent on a mission to kill me and my pack but they don't want to because of their morals so they going to help me!"

Oliver steps back in shock, eyes on me as Sebastian laughs.

"And you trust this Assassin?" Oliver questions.

"It's hard to explain man but I do trust it"

"Okay then I trust you so if you trust this Assassin then so do I" he looks at me asking if I got his message and I nod, loud and clear.

Going back i couldn't wait to see Cooper again but I ask Seb to drop me off at my house saying I'm going to grab some more clothes to stay at the pack house for a while which he agrees to and drops me off.

But instead I head to the Assassin compound in LA for some more missions as I had cleared mine."Death boss is on the phone for you" a cute girl walks in to the mission room.

I head to the meeting room and see there was a Skype call running and see Luca there.

"Angel! How's the mission going?"

"Good sir, I'm getting closer to them. It shouldn't be much longer now sir" I say calmly but my wolf whines.

"Fabulous just what I want to hear" he goes to end the call.

"Any news on my parents sir?" I question before he can end the call, his hand freezes by the end button.

He sighs "I'm afraid not Angel but I'm trying, you know that right? You trust me don't you?"

"Of course sir, thank you" He smiles but something seems off, but then he is strange anyway.

"Good girl" and with that he ends the call I sigh and head home to pack some clothes for the pack house.

Opening my locket I stare at their faces "don't worry, I'll find you! I promise".

Chapter 12 ~ Alpha Ares

The next few days were uneventful, we had fallen into this rou tine.He comes to my house at night time and we eat together and sleep in the same bed, in the morning he goes home to get ready to teach and then goes to the pack house after school to do any paper work before repeating it all over again.

Walking into English he looks up smelling my scent, he eyes look over my outfit which was a pair of jeans and an off the shoulder shirt before taking a deep breath and nodding to my seat making me chuckle.

In the middle of class I received a message.

Death Assassin

The next pack over from the Alpha Sebastian's has captured a young assassin. I want you to retrieve her and bring her back to me

Boss

I couldn't understand what his doing, we have separate assassins that do rescue missions. His also put me on a mission with someone who's just nosy, it's like his scared of something or someone so his using me to get jobs done.

The bell rings signalling lunch time.

"Miss Rose please stay behind" Sebastian says and everyone leaves ."Sebastian?" "Can you come with me to the pack house after school I need some help" he asks rubbing circles into my hand.

"Sure I'll meet you outside after school" nodding he kisses my hand letting me go eat.

After last lesson I make my way out and see Sebastian waiting for me "ready baby girl?"

Once in his office he sits me on his lap "I think it's time I'll tell you everything, I have been looking into a guy who calls himself the Boss. His been taking people in of all species and training them to be assassins but his reasons are selfish and dangerous." He runs his hands through my hair making my eyes close "he has caught on to me and sent the Death Assassin for me" I nod as his already told me this.

"The Alpha of a close pack has actually caught an Assassin and he told me she is his mate but his having problems with her and has asked me to come over, I don't think a girl who's scared of her own mate will want to talk to me so I was wondering if you'd come with me to help her?" He asks making my eyes open and he smiles sweetly kissing my forehead.

I nod and we head over to the pack, upon entering the pack grounds the Alpha comes to greet us.

"Alpha Sebastian thank you for coming I was getting worried, I'm Alpha Ares it's nice to finally meet you" he shakes Sebastian's hand.

"Alpha Ares it's a pleasure, I have brought my mate Angel to help us I hope you don't mind" he says introducing me.

I shake the Alphas hand saying hello and he shakes my hand smiling back.

"of course not, please this way"

Following him inside I look around it was a nice pack house, I had a feeling it was normally very clean but right now it was trashed.

Alpha Ares saw me looking around "sorry about the mess, she's feisty" I just laugh.

"So what's the problem Alpha?" I question still looking around before my eyes land on a silver axe, nice.

Walking over I rip it out of the wall and spin in round in my hands, light enough to handle but heavy enough to throw accurately.

I turn and see the Alpha looking at me in amusement.

"She threw that at my head, if I wasn't an Alpha I would have been dead and she's not talking to anyone"

"Can you please bring her down I'm sure I can help" he nods and heads upstairs.

Not long after there's screaming before a tall brunette comes flying down the stairs, upon seeing her I know who she is roughly as I had seen her before.

She spots me holding the axe and runs for me, Sebastian sees this and growls about to head over but I hold my hand up.

She pulls a knife from her boot and stands next to me ready to fight.

Sebastian sees this and raises an eyebrow but I just hold up the axe and shrug hoping he'd thing she thought I'd help because I was armed.

"Thank god you're here D...." I growl at her and pin her on the floor making her submit.

Alpha Ares growls slightly but Sebastian steps forward stopping his growl.

"Alpha can I please have a second to speak to her maybe I can talk her through it"

"Are you sure you'll be ok Angel?" Sebastian asks looking at the knife she just pulled from her boot.

"She just body slammed an Assassin that almost killed our Alpha I'm sure she'd be fine" another pack member from Alpha Ares pack said and they all left us be.

"What's going on?" I ask her and let her sit up."I was sent to find you but Alpha Ares caught me in a tree and he said we're mates"

"How you feel about that?" I ask her and she looks embarrassed.

"I like him, his so handsome and sweet but I know if Boss found out he'd kill me and him"

"It's ok I'll just tell him when I got here you had already been killed" I say looking at the axe.

"You'd do that for me?" Her eyes tear up.

"Yes I will, wait you said you were sent for me?" I question and she nods at the axe.

"That's for you Boss said he wanted you to slice the Alpha with that as it's infused with wolfsbane and liquid silver and bring the Alpha to him instead of killing him"

Well there went my plan to pretend to kill him

"Why would he do that?" I ask myself but she shrugs.

"His your mate isn't he?" She whispers.

"Yes he is"

"Are you going to kill him" she gasps.

"Never I just have to figure something out" she nods

"I can help you plus I'm happy I have someone to relate to" she looks down at her fingers.

"What's your name?"

"Louisa, I already your name is Angel" she smile and I smile back.

"You're going to be alright, you can trust Ares and I will tell Boss your dead"

"Thank you" she smiles hugging me as I pat her back and lead her out to Ares.

"You ok Princess?" Sebastian asks and I nod gesturing for Louisa to go to Ares.

She goes to him and hugs him like it was going to be the last time ever, he gasps and hugs her back.

After a while he looks up at me and steps towards me, he pulls me into a friendly hug.

"Thank you Angel, I will forever be in your debt" he whispers into my ear and I nod.

"Alpha Ares I understand that your grateful but my wolf can only be held back so long" Sebastian says gently bringing me to him.

"Excuse me Alpha how rude of me I'm just so grateful" he bows slightly.

"I understand no worries, now we should be on our way" he nods towards Louisa "if any of you need anything my pack is open"

Alpha Ares steps forward holding his hand out "as is mine" they shake hands and Louisa give me a hug goodbye before we go leave.

He drops me home saying how he needs to quickly do some pack work before coming back and I say goodbye.

Once inside I call Boss.

"Hello?" He answers the phone impatiently.

"Boss it's Angel, I went to the pack and she was dead in the cells but they had burnt the body already I'm sorry I couldn't retrieve her"

"Of course don't worry Angel don't worry about killing them it's her own fault for being caught. I must ask though did you find an axe?" He question.

"I did and I also found a note explaining why I have the axe" I explain.

"Good she wasn't completely useless then, well if that's all I'll send the money into your bank"

"Yes sir" and with that he hangs up and I get a notification about the money.

How cheery.

Chapter 13 ~ going back

It was almost my two month mark and I was beginning to panic, I haven't gotten closer to working how to fix this.

Me and Sebastian had gotten closer and multiple times his tried to make moves but I told him I'm just not ready yet which he has been so respectful.

Me and the group have gotten closer and they're all like brothers and sisters to me now there's no way I'd kill or allow anyone else to kill them.

Getting ready to go to the pack house I get a notification from Boss, Shit this is it his telling me his sending another assassin.

Opening my phone I look at the text and frown.

Dear Death Assassin,

We have a problem. While you've been on your mission we have been having loads of problems back here at the corporation.

We need you back immediately, Don't worry i will put your mission on hold and you can go back and finish that as i have no one as trusted to finish it and i know you like finishing what you started.

There is an Alpha not far from here who is planning on attacking us in two weeks time you can tell your mission you're going to visit a sick parent or whatever you think will work.

i expect you back in 48 hours we won't stand this without you.

Boss.

I couldn't use the sick parent thing because I already told him they were gone and I had no other relatives so in the morning I'll just have to tell them I need to go back to Texas.

Going to the pack house I spend the whole day with them and Cooper but I can tell they feel like somethings off.

That night they were acting as though they all knew I was leaving.

In the morning I gather them all in the kitchen as I make them breakfast.

"Right what the fuck is going on!" Zoey says saying what was on everyone's mind.

I sigh and hand out their plates in silence.

"Angel don't pretend you're deaf" she glares at me and I sit down.

"I'm going back to Texas" I say taking a mouthful of food.

William frowns, Zoey freezes, Niko chokes on his mouthful, summer starts crying and Sebastian just growls yanking me into his lap.

"If you think I'm letting you leave you have another thing coming" he snarls into my neck.

"Why would you leave us" summer whimpers making William take her into his arms.

"I have to otherwise a lot of people are going to die" I say leaving no room for arguments.

Zoey starts laughing making everyone look at her "funny one Angel now sit and eat your fucking food, it's too early for jokes" she glares at me.

"I'm being serious Zoey I leave in a few hours and that's final" I state making Sebastian growl, the whole kitchen shakes.

"So you're telling me you're leaving us to go to Texas in a few hours?" Niko slows the sentence down.

"Yes"

"No" Niko says and carries on eating like nothing happened.

"What do you mean no? I'm leaving and that's it" I say getting off of Sebastian's lap and run home to begin packing.

As I'm packing I hear my front door slam open making me roll my eyes.

"You can't leave Angel" William says as they all step into my room.

"Is it something we did?" Summer whispers looking at me with wide eyes.

I sigh and stop packing hugging her "no Sum I just have to leave for a little bit, I promise I'll come back, have I ever broken one of my promises?"

She shakes her head " I need to go for a few days that's all"

"We'll go with you then" Zoey says placing her hands on her hips willing me to argue with her.

"And leave the pack unprotected?" I simply say and she glares at me.

"I'll go with you then" she growls making Niko hug her before she bursts out crying.

"Please don't leave Angel, I have a bad feeling about this. If you go you won't come back" she sobs making the boys growl.

"I'm sorry Zo I need to go please I promise I'll be fine. Plus I need someone to look after Cooper" I smile gently.

William stands straighter "you're leaving Cooper here?" He questions and I know it's because they know I'd never leave him here and never come back for him.

I nod and they reluctantly leave with the girls sobbing " I swear Angel if you don't come back I'll find you and shave your hair off" Zoey says before leaving.

The only person who didn't leave was Sebastian.

"Please don't go" he whispers silent tears falling from his eyes.

"I'm sorry Seb but I have to, you don't understand. I'll be back in a few days I promise" I gently wipe his tears away "I want to be with you Sebastian and the only way to do that is hopefully for me to go"

He nods "I get it but it doesn't make this any better" he hugs me to him breathing in my scent.

"I know" I whisper as he look up at me.

"Can I kiss you?" He whispers looking at my lips.

We haven't kissed yet because I didn't want to get too attached but it's too late now I guess. So I just nod leaning forward.

He leans forward and his lips meet mine.

Millions of tiny spark followed that little action, it was warm and it felt right.

We didn't move just stayed there gently kissing each other with so much love I knew from then on I'd die for this man. I'd kill for him and if I have to I'll kill Boss.

After a little while I gently remove my lips from his and place my head in the crook of his neck breathing his scent in.

"I'm going to make this work, for us" I say and look up at him before pressing one final bruising kiss on his lips.

Unlocking myself from him I grab my bag and walk out of my house, that was the single most hardest thing I'd ever have to do.

Sebastian POV ~

And just like that she left, taking my heart with her.I couldn't find it in myself to leave her house and Cooper laid at my feet just watching me.

Having long stopped crying by now, glancing at her bedside table the clock showed it was 18:36 she'd been gone for eight hours and would be on the plane by now.

I couldn't believe I'd been sat here for eight hours, still not understanding why she left I decided to look around to see what spooked her.

Checking her table, draw and bathroom I didn't find anything so I decided to move to her wardrobe.

Again nothing frustrated I push all her clothes to one side and see a small hole in the back of her wardrobe.

"What the hell?" in shock I pull the hole and it slide to one side revealing a whole panel of cameras showing the whole inside and outside of her house, there was also some weapons.

Sitting on her bed i start thinking about what she had said.

Running back to the pack house with Cooper in tow, I knew something was up i just have to find out what.

Chapter 14 ~ Alpha Gabriel

After the 18 hour flight I was tired but I was in Texas now and didn't have time to waste so I head straight to the compound.

Everyone was running around worried, some were crying, some looked ready to be sick but when I walked in it was like everyone took a deep breath to relax.

"Angel in here" boss shouts from his office.Walking in I see him in his chair, his blonde hair looked greasy like he hasn't had time to shower, his brown eyes were bloodshot and his eye bags looked deep.

"I need to update you on everything" taking a seat he pulls out a file."This is Alpha Gabriel, I'm sure you know how he's the only Alpha in Texas. He is the most feared Alpha because his killed over 200 rouges in a space of two weeks after they killed his Luna"

He rolled his eyes.

"So why is he trying to take out an organization who kills rouges?" I question looking at the photo placed in front of me.

The man have black hair with a thick black beard, his eyes were silver and cold they held no warmth and his mouth was pulled in a sneer.

"His pack has over 500 wolves and 300 of those are fighters making his pack the biggest pack in the world" he carries out ignoring my question but I can see why everyone's worried.

"So why is he after you?" I laugh finding the slight panic coming off of him amusing.

Boss freaks out shouting "They're not after me you stupid girl! Why would you even suggest such a thing?" He screams making me raise an eyebrow.

Calming down he clears his throat "you need to go spy on them"

"That's not my job" standing up I go to walk out.

"I don't care, go spy on them" he shouts after me but i just rolls my eyes and leave.

"Not like there's anything better to do anyway" I shout back and head out.

I made it to the Alpha's office faster then I thought with the help of the six pack fighters carrying me in.

"Alpha, look who we found snooping around just like he said" one laughs and the Alpha signals them to sit me down I just stay seated not moving, I needed to assess the situation I was in, there's no way they would have found me like that and who was he?

"Alpha" I greet him but he just chuckles.

"Death Assassin or shall I call you Angel? You can call me Gabriel"

Shocked I just sat there speechless.

"I want you to know that your 'Boss' basically sold you to us to get us to stop attacking him because he believed we wanted to kill you but actually we want you on our side"

"What do you mean?" I snort this was ridiculous, there's no way he would have done that, I was pretty much his only hope and he knew that.

"He has been lying to you for years! Now Angel I have sent Alpha Sebastian an email and I'm guessing he is your mate considering he isn't dead yet, hopefully he will be here in a few days or so because I have big plans but I'll allow your mate to explain' Alpha Gabriel say waving his arms up, he looked like the picture Boss sent me but his hair was longer and his eyes not so cold and he had a set expression that he knew a secret no one else did.

"ill let my men show you to a room, no harm will come to you here Angel and I hope we can get to know each other better, it would be nice to have you on our side. I can tell you're a good person but I'm not stupid, you're dangerous" he leans back running a hand over his beard he gets a distant look on his face.

"Take a wolf from it's pack, get it to protect you, do your dirty work is one thing but to then corner it?" he chuckles his silver eyes snapping to me still holding the distant look, it was like he was looking right through me "Any animal would turn feral after that and a feral animal is a dangerous one" Shaking his head like he was clearing his thoughts he waved to a pack member who brought me in "I'll be seeing you soon Angel"

I was shown to a room after that little show my head still spinning, jumping into the shower I try to clear my head. How could he have sold me to a pack I thought he said he needed me? What did Alpha Gabriel mean take a wolf from it's pack?

Doesn't Boss realize if I died and they carried on with the attack everyone would die? Traitor!

And how the hell did this Alpha know my name?

Chapter 15 ~ Luca O'Connor

Sebastian's POV ~

After almost two days of my beautiful mate being gone I finally decide to do some work to take my mind off of everything, opening my email I sit straighter when I see an email from Texas.

Alpha Sebastian,

This is Alpha Gabriel, I am contacting you due to your research, I know about the Assassins and their leader. I also happen to know where they are situated as my Beta's mate was one of their Assassin's however she was killed when they found out and I have reasons to believe that he is the reason my mate is dead.

My beta's mate told us about all of the Assassin's and the building before she died. All I can tell you is that the building is situated about twenty miles from my pack.

They call the leader The Boss as no one knows his real name but I do know that he has been known to go by the name Luca O'Conn or...I know why this should come as a shock to you.

Also I wanted to let you know that they have been coming on to my territory so I have been planning an attack in about two weeks time, I do know that they will have the famous Death Assassin even though I have heard she is up by you, I have no doubt about it that she will be there, so I am emailing you to ask if you can accompany my pack in the attack and I also have a lot of information I think you would like to know about Angel Rose.

You are invited to my pack hopefully sooner rather then later.

But if not and if me and my whole pack dies I would like you to take over my land and finish this arsehole for good.

Kind regards Alpha Gabriel

I can't believe what what I was seeing, either this was a whole big coincidence or my beautiful mate was the Death Assassin.

and why Luca O'Connor?

I needed to get up there.

A day later me and most of my pack were in Texas about to walking on to Alpha Gabriel's pack, my mother and father were called back to protect and lead the pack member who stayed home.

"Stop where you are!" A man steps forward.

"I'm Alpha Sebastian, I got an email for your Alpha"

"Of course Alpha sorry I'll let him know you're here" the pack fighter stepped down allowing me and my pack past mind linking his Alpha I was there.

"Alpha Sebastian" Alpha Gabriel says holding his hand out, i had been told about Alpha Gabriel by my dad but I'd never seen him as when i came into position of my Alpha title his Luna was taken from him and he hasn't been to any Alpha meetings just emails.

The stories were true, his eyes pure silver the mark of a strong wolf who has lost their mate too soon, the moon goddess takes pity on these wolves and allows an even stronger bond between man and wolf bring forward the silver coloring of our bond strings, bonding us together. It's not real silver but it's to show the bond is still pure and stronger than most.

"Pleasure to meet you Alpha" I greet him shaking his hand.

"I'm Alpha Gabriel, its nice to meet you finally, please" he waves towards the building and we all follow him inside. "So I know you're probably wondering why I sent you that email, I know your mate Angel"

My wolf growls lowly and Alpha Gabriel puts his hands up "She's here if you want me to call her, you two have a lot to talk about anyway but I knew we needed her on our side and if she carried on like this there would be a lot of people dead" with that he nods to a pack member to go get Angel.

"What are you talking about my mate wouldn't hurt a fly" My wolf Lynx takes over.

"No she wouldn't have if what happened to her was differently but she does hurt people, actually worse but that's her story to tell"

Angel walks in and I immediately run to her lifting her into my arms hugging her to me like she'd disappear, Lynx slowly slipping back letting me take control.

Putting her down I look at her "Angel your eyes?" I take a step back.

"Woah, how do you keep getting even better looking" Zoey yells and attacks Angel in a hug "I told you I'd come" I was still in shock and apparently so was everyone else but Zoey.

"I was right" Alpha Gabriel laughs "But I pretty much always am" he gives a cheeky smirk shocking me, everyone talks about this man and how cold he is after losing his Luna and here he was joking and smirking.

"Angel I'm sure you'd like to start this off" Alpha Gabriel smiles gently to my mate, Lynx growls but I know there was nothing romantic behind it, losing your soulmate the way he did has a way with bring man and wolf closer but in doing so the bond to the mate becomes stronger, even though his mate is gone he still loves her too much to even stomach looking at another female in that way.

"Right we all need to have a serious talk" Angel says and I sit down with her in my lap, she smiles at Niko and William. Summer stayed back at the pack to help with the females and kids as she was the Beta female.

"So you know the story with my parents but I left some bits out" she starts, holding her hand above my heart kissing my cheek.

She's so beautiful, take her now! In front of everyone we have to show them she's ours! lynx growls trying to push forward "No you silly wolf now listen to our mate"

"When my mother placed me into our hideout she told me to look for her old Alpha Luca O'Conner but Luca found me instead and he wasn't an Alpha at the time but he owned the Assassin company so he was the Alpha so to speak. He took me and trained me into being an Assassin, I was assigned to take out your pack but I just couldn't and I'm sorry about the contacts its a must when taking a cover, I'm also sorry I didn't tell you sooner. I was just scared you'd all hate me because I'm a monster"

"You're not a monster Angel, I understand how it feels to lose you parents" Zoey speaks up "my father was killed by this Boss man because he overheard some Assassins talking about some rouge who killed a child trying to be trained by you. I went on a rampage, I killed everything in sight. If you're a monster then so am I" she smiles gently at Angel getting up she grabs Angels hand squeezing it.

"She didn't" I whisper looking in her blue eyes, I can't believe I didn't notice she was wearing contacts.

I thought she was perfect before but once I saw her eyes my wolf howls at her beauty, she definitely looked like an Angel.

Her eyes were a dark blue around the edges with the prettiest shade of blue in the center that looked like the clearest water but it had spots of hazel and golds which got lighter or darker depending on lighting and her emotions.

Fucking stunning! Lynx purrs and I agreed I can't wait to mark her "Me neither bud" I sigh now was not the time.

"What?" She tilted her head to the side in confusion.

"Your mother wasn't mistaken about Luca O'Conner" I gently pushing her white hair to the side trying to find the best way to find her.

"She didn't mix him up because Luca O'Conner is my father".

Chapter 16 ~ Polaroids

Sebastian's POV ~

I tell her the full story that I know.

"My dad heard that old pack members were in trouble from this guy that had a few assassins at the time and was looking to take down anyone who tried stopping him, he wanted to take over all the packs and become king of the Alpha's even thought he wasn't a werewolf." She nods for me to continue eyes glistening with unshed tears.

"My dad tried to find his pack members but when he did all he found was this remote house that was burned but still intact, they didn't find any bodies so he thought that they were still alive.In the house they found signs of a child which he assumed is why they wanted to leave, they made him sign a contract that he would never tell anyone about them and he signed it and erased the packs memory of them, his been looking for them ever since" she cuddles into my chest more

"He never told anyone their names as they wanted to go into hiding but he did tell me their last names"

"Which were?" She tenses.

"The Blackwoods" I look into her eyes "Your parents?" I ask and she nods.

"My full name is Angel Rose Blackwood"

She starts crying "so what are you trying to say exactly?"

"Basically you have been working with the guy that took your parents" Alpha Gabriel snorts at the irony.

Both me and Angel turn to him with glares

"What it's true" he shrugs.

"So my parents are still alive?" She asks Alpha Gabriel who seemed to know everything.

"We believe he has been keeping them in a basement" he says making eye contact with one of his member who stepped forward with polaroid photos of a dingy basement and two people, I didn't even need to see their faces there was two people hugging all you saw was a big guy holding a small lady with stark white hair.

Angel starts panicking but I calm her down.

"Alright I'm going to call him and tell him we've killed you but we're still going to attack this will give us the upper hand as he'll believe you dead" Alpha Gabriel after a long time of silence.

Picking the phone up he dials Bosses number and puts it on speaker holding a finger to his lips.

"Hello?" a slightly high pitched mans voice breaks the silence.

"Deals off, we killed the girl but you see she wasn't the problem, you are. I had to get rid of her first to decrease deaths on my side" Alpha Gabriel chuckles "how stupid are you?"

"No! We had a deal! You kill her and stop the attack" the guy screams down the phone.

"And now I'm telling you the deals off and we're coming for you" Alpha Gabriel then hangs up.

We start planning an attack "There's a huge clearing not far from the compound, they go there a lot for practice" Angel points at a map.

"Good we'll wait till they're training, will he be there?" Gabriel asks her and Angel nods. "How about the others will they surrender?"

"No, they're terrified of him the only way they'll surrender is if his killed, but he'll hide behind them before that happens" Angel shakes her head pinching the bridge of her nose and everyone nods.

"Well we will wait in hiding until they train, once we have eyes on him we'll move in and try to kill him before there's too many deaths" Gabriel states looking at Angel for approval.

"We can bring some of my warriors over here and I'll contact Alpha Ares to bring a few of his here but if it's ok with you they can stay here and be ready for a surprise attack or wounded?" I question Alpha Gabriel.

"Good idea, you call your warriors, I'll get Alpha Ares on the phone and Alpha Gabriel you tell your warriors about our plan" Angel steps forward and everyone started moving.

Sorry for the short chapter

Chapter 17 ~ Trauma

Angels POV

Two days later we are in hiding at the clearing waiting for training to start.Looking around I see about three hundred wolves both Sebastian's pack and Alpha Gabriel's waiting for the word.

Some of them looked eager while others looked weary.

We had been here for two hours now watching them train for the impending attack but no sign of boss, until hour three a warrior nudged me and pointed to the right.

Squinting I put my hand in the air signaling for everyone to get ready, nodding to both Sebastian and Alpha Gabriel they nod and they mind link their packs to attack.

We had already planned that the boys were going to fight while me and a handful of warriors were going to head to the basement.

The building was a mess, it looked like a tornado had blown through "this way guys" I whisper in case there's assassins left in here.

I knew where the basement was as he used to take rouges down there to question them but no one else was allowed down.

We all proceeded with caution and came to the large steel door with a code for entrance.

"How are we going to get in?" One of the guys asked."The boss isn't very smart so just try 1234 on the code" and just like I had suggested the door flashed green and we pulled it open.

There was a spiral staircase leading down, walking down the guy in front of me walks in to the open space.

It took my eyes a second to adjust to the darkness, there were endless cages. All holding two or more people.

They were all terrified, slamming their bodies up against the walls furthest away from us.

"Break them all out" was all I needed to say before everyone started breaking the cages apart wearing gloves so the bars didn't burn, it wreaked of wolfsbane, silver and burnt skin.

While they were coaxing the people out of the cages I waked past each cage looking at everyone.Reaching the end of cages I lost hope, they wasn't here.

Growling I ripped the closest cages door off the hinges, the silver burning my palms but I was numb.

"They're behind the wall" a gruff voice calls to me, turning to the cage I broke apart there sat a old man, white tangled beard and hair, brown eyes and tatted clothes.

"Excuse me?"

"The lady with hair white as yours and a big man with eyes like yours" his coughs at the use of his voice "they're behind a hidden door in the wall" shakily he shuffles forward taking my arm, pulling me to the end of the hall he taps on the wall.

"Thank you" I motion a warrior over to him "this man is going to get you out of here, we have medical help where we are stationed" but he just stares at me.

"I won't make it" he smiles sadly.

"What do you mean? We'll help you, don't worry" the warrior stepped forward, however, the mans eyes didn't leave mine.

"You don't understand, sometimes memories are the worst form of torture." His eyes fill with tears becoming misty.

"How much fear, pain and trauma do you think one can take before they're willing to let the love of their life take the punishment, just to get some relief?" Breathing becoming shallow, a stray tear falls.

No one says anything and the silence was deafening.

"Years of it, 20 years in fact" he looked back into the cage as if looking for someone."20 years of torture and I broke, she could only take one day and it killed her."

My breath caught in my throat as he makes eye contact again with me and then looked at the warrior.

"I'm not making it out of this cellar son because I don't want to live with out my Hannah. Now you need to get behind that wall"

He steps back into his cage and sat down, I walk up to the wall and push.

It swung outward revealing one lone cage, inside that cage were my parents.

"Oh my god! Mom! Dad!" Running forward to rip the cage doors off the cage.

"Angel no!" My dad coughed and I yell in pain as my skin makes contact with the bars.

Silver laced with wolfsbane, he really must have wanted to keep them and others out of this one as the rest of the cages are just steel laced with wolfsbane.

Growling I step forward again "Angel, don't you dare" my dad growls at me using the wall for balance he stands up as much as he could.

Latching onto the bars I hiss but I continue to pull, the bars not moving.

"Angel stop" my mother whispers her voice breaking.

"No" growling I let Athena take over, thinking about all the time they've been under my nose and I've been working for that scum, how beaten my dad looked, how broken my mother seemed.

Athena lets out a roar and finally the bars started groaning before they finally gave way, my hands were burnt real bad but they would start healing soon.

Running forward I embrace them both "we need to go"

Me and another warrior helped them up the stairs, once we got to the top I immediately see fights and notice we're winning.

"Take them to the medics I'm going to help everyone" the warrior nods and starts moving them.

Looking out in the field I see him and he's already looking at me, his nostrils flaring, eyes lit with rage.

Smirking I step forward trying to antagonize him, which worked.

He starts sprinting towards me, growling I lunge when his close enough taking us both to the ground.

For a human his pretty well skilled but in the end wolf strength will always win.

I throw him back a few feet, his body soaring through the air until he lands with a sickening thud.

However, he gets up grabbing a bow from a fallen assassin to fast for me to comprehend.

Cocking the arrow he lets it fly.

Chapter 18 ~ Brings Out Your Eyes

Before the arrow that was aimed for my heart hit me, someone forced me to the ground.

The sound of someone's body hitting the ground forces me out of my shock.

Looking over I see my father with his eyes shut, blood trail on his forehead from a previous hit and an arrow out of his mid back.

It's like the world froze and time just stopped, my ears were ringing and it felt like I was drowning. All I could hear was someone screaming so hard some wolves dropped to their knees holding their ears.

It wasn't until my ears stopping ringing I realized it was me who was screaming.

It was all my fault, he died because of me, he died because I was weak, I was slow, I was worthless.

I had just got him back.

Standing up I look down at his body, his eyes still closed unmoving, I look up and see the boss just standing there with a smug look on his face.

Walking forward everything goes blurry apart from him, it was like tunnel vision.

He starts firing arrows at me, I either dodge or snap them all slowly not stopping my slow pace forward.

Other assassins tried attacking my on my travel but without pausing I either ripped their heads off or stabbed them in the hearts with an arrow he launched at me.

Once he saw he wasn't hitting me and no one could stop me from moving forwards he slowly starts backing up planning on running like a dog with his tail between his legs. But Zoey approaches like a lioness, stealthy and slick she grabs his arms from behind holding him there for me.

Walking in front of him I just stop and look at his face still numb and he starts begging.

"Please don't do this, I kept you alive all this time, I trained you how you are now! You would be weak without me!"

Zoey laughs at his attempts "You look cute with all that blood on you, it brings out your eyes" she says to me.

Smirking I thrust my hand forward into his stomach and set my hand on fire slowly burning him from inside out.

"Oh I didn't know we were having a barbecue, sweet" she growls in blood hunger making me snicker, at this point we were both switched off. There were no rights or wrongs, nothing was too far.

The only thing that matter was his pain and getting justice for the people he hurt"

He starts fighting in Zoey's arms but she pins him still against her, her eyes holding rage for my dad who was killed just like hers at his hands, her pupils fully dilated as if she was getting high off this feeling.

"Stop" he said, his breath ragged "Please"

Instead of talking to him I look at Zoey "How you feeling?"

She snickers "Well now that you ask, I'd be fine but his writhing is so inconsiderate! It takes a fair amount of effort holding him still you know?"

"Oh dear, should I stop him moving?" I chuckle as he pleads.

She looks at me and smirks nodding "Girl after my own heart..."

"Perfect" I appreciate her thinking.

I retreat my hand and force my hand into his Chest cavity gently holding his heart in my hand, his eyes begin to drop but before he passes out I light his heart on fire and he screams before I take my hand out with his heart turning in to ashes in my hand.

Zoey steps back and allows his body to drop, eyes never leaving mine.

"Angel" someone screams my name and I turn finding my mum standing over someone's body.

Not just anyone's body.

Sebastian.

Chapter 19 ~ Sunshine

Running forward I slide to my knees grabbing hold of him.

"It's ok! You're going to be ok! Everything's fine!" My voice on the verge of breaking as I shakily run my hands over him my feelings slowly coming back.

"Angel he needs help now" my mother cries looking at my fathers body before looking back at Sebastian.

"His been hit with too many wolfsbane bullets"

"How" I frown down at him.

"When you were going to kill him people were shooting at you but he took the bullets." She whispers looking at me.

I refuse to lose someone else because they tried to save me.

"You're so stupid" I cry at him running my finger over his cheeks leaving blood trails, I start to panic trying to wipe it off but it gets worse.

He laughs and coughs up blood "You're so beautiful"

"We're going to get you help ok" I say forgetting about his face, I start putting pressure to his stomach.

"Please do this isn't fun" he winces and I cry laugh.

"Actually I need you to look after something for me ok? You need to give it back to me after ok?" I plead.

He nods "always" he groans eyes slowly closing.

"Sebastian! You haven't even seen what it is" I cry and he smiles.

I place it in his hand and he looks at it and cries, "You kept it?" He cries holding the key he made for my house to his chest.

"Always but you have to give it back when your better, promise?" I cry.

"I promise"

"I love you" "I love you too" he grunts, eyes flickering closed."Plea se...please don't close your eyes!" I beg but his eyes close.

He passes out but his chest still rises and falls.

"Angel his breathing!" Someone shouts behind me.

I turn and see William with a hand to my fathers neck, My mother runs across the field faster then i thought possible and checks for herself, she cries looking up she nods her head to me.

"There's a pulse but is too weak we need to go now Angel" she sobs and William lifts my fathers body running to the pack hospital.

Alpha Gabriel comes forward and lifts Sebastian and he rushes him to the pack hospital with the others, Zoey and I stay with some warriors to check the fallen and check the building. We gather all our fallen allies to be transported back for a burial, we only found 10.

"Angel you need to go back, check on them" Zoey says with her hand on my shoulder, her face was hard but I knew she was worried, no one had heard anything about Niko. "I've got it covered here".

Once I make it to Alpha Gabriel's pack I was greeted by Alpha Ace.

"Angel!" He shouts sprinting to me as though I'm hurt, it doesn't make sense until I remember Zoey's comment about the blood.

"It's not mine, where my dad and Seb" I question him.

"Alpha Seb is in surgery to remove the bullets and your dad is with your mum in recovery, you can see him once we get you checked and cleaned" he starts taking me by the shoulders and moving me into the building.

"No take me straight to them"

"But..."

"Please Alpha, I need to see him" I look up at him.

He huffs handing me a cloth "At least wipe your face you bloody cave woman" Rolling his eyes he leads me to the recovery section.

Once we reached the room he told me he was going to check on some wolves that got hurt.

Walking in I storm right up to my dad "What the hell was that! I only just found you guys after 12 years and you pull some stupid trick like that!"

My mum stepped forward "Angel please"

"No! You don't get to do that! You don't get to leave right after I found you!" At this point I'm crying and shouting at the same time.

"You were meant to come straight here! What was you even still doing there!"

My dad doesn't say anything just stands up and walks over to me.

"What are you doing! Answer me!"

Without a word he pulls me into his chest, he was roughly the same height as Seb but his hug was different it was more warm, it felt like I was 6 again.

It felt like back home.

I broke down and he still has yet to say anything, he just holds me. Running his fingers through my hair then he holds my head against his chest.

"Did you really think I was going to sit back and watch my daughter get hit by an arrow?"

"Dad..." I start trying to pull back.

His hold was firm "no you will listen to me Angel, I am your father! I am meant to protect you, that's what I did that night and today and what I'll do for the rest of my life" his hold on me tightens.

"Don't you dare think that because we were there for so long we are weak, and you now need to protect us! No matter what, I am your protector. From the day you were born until I die and if that means dying to protect you I'd do it over and over without question"

"But I don't want you to die, I've only just got you back" I sob.

He laughs sadly "I was never gone. In life or death, if I'm there or not. I will always be in here" he pulls back and points to my heart "I was never gone Princess"

"I've done terrible things Daddy" I whimper my emotions hitting me full force.

My mother step forward running her knuckles gently across my cheek "We all have sunshine, you didn't understand. You were so young, so trusting, so innocent and you will never be blamed for what you did."

Before I got a chance to correct her there was a knock on the door and Alpha Ace stepped inside.

"Angel, they've finished working in Alpha Sebastian, you can see him but he'll most likely be asleep"

"Thank you Alpha" I nod.

"Pfft please, just Ace" then he leaves, leaving us to our moment.

"Alpha Sebastian huh?" My father questions.

"Oh he's handsome!" My mother adds nodding her head approvingly.

"First my princess, now my queen? I think I need to put this child in his place" he puffs his chest out.

"Oh dear please stop, you look constipated" My mother pats his chest before turning to me "Well what are you waiting for, we'll be here. Go get him sunshine"

After a while of making sure they wasn't going to disappear the need to see my mate got too much.

Reaching his room I step inside, he was already awake.

"Hey" I whisper and he smile weakly, stepping forward I walk to his bed and sit on the chair but he shakes his head.

"What? What's wrong!" I start panicking but he clears his throat.

"Please lay with me" and he slowly moves his body to the far side of the bed wincing slightly.

"I don't want to..."

"Please" he pleads and with that I gently lower my body on the bed.

We don't touch but we just lay side by side looking at each other.

"You're stupid"

"And you're beautiful"

Neither of us speak, we just lay silently enjoying each other's company.

I don't even remember when we fell asleep.

I wake up to a nurse checking his wounds on his back.

"Oh hi, sorry if I woke you" she smiles gently.

"How is he?" I ask shaking my head.

"Fantastic, I think spending the night in such close proximity of his mate sped up his healing, his almost fully healed. It will probably take a few days until his back to full strength due to the wolfsbane but he's doing very well" She steps back moving towards the door "I'll leave you in peace"

Once she was gone I turn to Seb and almost scream when I see him already looking at me.

"Sped up my healing yeah?" He wiggles his eyebrows.

"Yep, you're fine" I laugh sitting up.

"No" he fake winces "See! Still hurt, come back"

"Well seeing as you're better, you have something to give me?" I jokingly ask.

He chucks the key to me "You can have it but you won't be needing it" He sighs sitting up against the pillows.

"And why's that?"

"You're moving into the pack house" he says with certainty.

This time though I don't argue.

I don't even want to.

CPSIA information can be obtained
at www.ICGtesting.com
Printed in the USA
LVHW040111060123
736479LV00011B/981

9 781837 616640